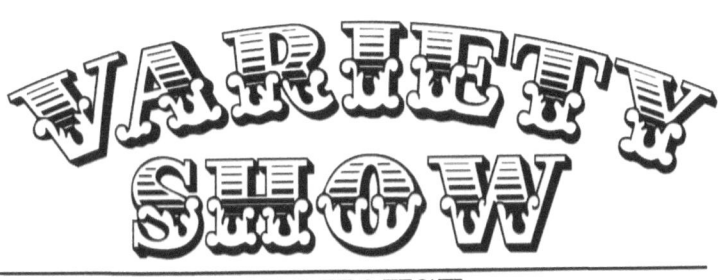

ALI HOUSE

THE ENGEN UNIVERSE

Published in Canada by Engen Books, St. John's, NL.

Library and Archives Canada Cataloguing in Publication

Title: Variety show / Ali House.
Names: House, Ali, 1982- author.
Description: Sequel to: Jacobi Street.
Identifiers: Canadiana (print) 20210117176 | Canadiana (ebook) 20210117265 |
ISBN 9781774780107
  (softcover) | ISBN 9781774780114 (PDF)
Classification: LCC PS8615.O867 V37 2021 | DDC C813/.6—dc23

Distributed by:
Engen Books
www.engenbooks.com
submissions@engenbooks.com

First mass market paperback printing: February 2021

Cover Image: Ellen Curtis

For all you theatre nerds.

And for Matthew,
who created such a great world
that I had to steal it.

CHAPTER ONE

"You hear that?"

Francesca didn't bother turning to look at the thin man to her left, but she did roll her eyes at his question. "Hear what?" she asked in a bored voice. They had been standing in the off-right wing for the past fifteen minutes, waiting for their scene to finally start rehearsing, and she hadn't heard anything other than the director angrily giving instructions to the set designer on how to hang the moon. It was a scene that everyone at the theatre was well versed in, as it happened at least four times during every stumble-through. Jim, the director, would find some fault in the set or lights and instead of communicating it in English, he would give all his instructions in French, knowing full well that Billy, the set and lighting designer and resident stagehand, couldn't understand him. Billy would then politely ask Jim to speak in English, and the mere suggestion would cause Jim to fume angrily for at least a minute before reluctantly replying in English.

Watching such a scene was an entertaining enough way to pass the time while waiting for rehearsal to continue, but as Jim continued to fret over the precise location of the wooden moon, Francesca began to wonder if she and Gerard would be standing here forever.

"Hear *that*," Gerard repeated.

Sighing, Francesca turned to him, wishing that he'd put out that damn cigarette. The scent reminded her of days and nights spent on the smoke-filled verandas of Paris, drinking with famous actors and directors, and right now it wasn't a memory the large blonde woman wanted to revisit.

Before she could speak, he put one finger up to his lips, the tip of which rested under his large, hooked nose, indicating for her to be quiet. She glared at him, which he pretended not to notice. Moving backwards, he stepped away from the stage and further into the wing. He was careful to step around the prop-tables, costume racks, and set pieces that were cluttering the area. By tomorrow everything would be neatly placed and easy to manoeuvre around, but right now the area was more akin to an obstacle course set up by drunkards.

As Gerard moved further away from the stage, the director's cursing grew more distant, until it was barely noticeable. Once he was far enough back, he listened and waited. For a long moment there was nothing, and then there was a sound, a low, deep knocking sound that seemed to come from the depths of the theatre.

Gesturing for her to come join him, he watched as Francesca reluctantly came over. After another moment, the sound repeated itself. She raised an eyebrow. "Do you think something's gotten in the pipes?"

Gerard frowned and paused to think. "It's probably something to do with the furnace," he said dismissively, taking a puff from the cigarette he carelessly held in his right hand. Now that the mystery had been solved, he'd instantly lost interest. Was it too much to ask that something *interesting* happen in this theatre?

"Perhaps you should make yourself useful and go fix it," Francesca shot at him.

"You shouldn't be smoking back here," a nasally voice called out.

Gerard rolled his eyes at the intrusion. "It's only a cigarette, Scott."

The young, red-headed man stepped out from behind a large set piece and tried to glare at Gerard through his bottle-thick glasses. Unfortunately, the effect wasn't anywhere close to what he was hoping to achieve.

"He has a point," Francesca remarked, using her hand to wave the smoke away from her face. "And if Ari sees you, they'll tear a strip off you. You're in costume, after all."

The threat of the stage manager's wrath was enough to make Gerard second-guess his obstinate determination to break all the theatre's rules. However, he was not going to show weakness in front of a lackey like Scott. Taking a long drag, he smirked at the young man before blowing smoke in his direction.

Scott coughed and tried to wave the smoke away with his clipboard. "Monsieur Le Faull says that we'll be starting the 'Amore' sketch in two minutes, so be ready."

"Just call him Jim," Gerard said impatiently. "Everyone else does."

Scott clenched his jaw and exited through the door, heading to the green room to warn the other actors.

"What an annoying little twerp," Gerard muttered to himself. He waited until Scott was out of sight before putting his cigarette out on the back of a nearby set piece and slipping the unfinished portion into his pocket.

"Do you think you'll remember your lines this time?" Francesca remarked as she smoothed her costume, her pleasant pitch tinged with hostility.

"Francesca, please," he said, putting on his most flattering tone. "Shall we have this tiresome conversation all over again? You know I always get it right by the night of the show."

She crossed her arms over her ample chest. Despite the many years she'd worked with Gerard, she had yet to get accustomed to his various "methods." He claimed that it was part of his routine to never say his lines correctly until there was an audience in the house, but she knew that he was bluffing around his terrible memory. Perhaps if he spent more time with his script and less time with a certain young actress...

The knocking sounded again, but this time it was louder and sharper.

"Are you sure it's the furnace?" Francesca asked, resisting the urge to glance towards the backstage door.

"Probably," Gerard shrugged. "What else could it be?"

She didn't know why the noise unnerved her, but it did. "I swear I've never heard it do anything like this before. Do you think something's wrong with it?"

"Perhaps you should concentrate less on the furnace and more on the skit we'll be doing in a few seconds, once *le Director* stops cursing."

"Gerard, please," she scoffed. "Of the two of us, I'm *never* the least prepared. All I'm suggesting is that maybe someone should go back there and make sure the furnace isn't about to explode."

He rolled his eyes. "It's likely nothing."

"But maybe it is."

"But maybe it's not."

"Maybe it's a ghost!"

Both of them jumped at the sudden exclamation.

"*Merde*," Francesca swore under her breath as she turned around to see two young women standing behind her, both dressed in black pants and white shirts, their hair pulled back into ponytails. Despite their similar costumes, the two women looked nothing alike, with the taller of the two having dark skin and curly black hair, and the shorter having pale skin and long brown hair. It was Stacey, the taller woman, who'd startled them, and her lips parted in a wide smile as she relished how she'd managed to spook the two elder actors. The other, Wendy, managed to keep her face neutral, but there was the slightest hint of amusement in her eyes.

Francesca hadn't heard either of them approach and resented the fact that she'd been startled this close to performing. This kind of thing never would have happened in Paris—the ensemble would have known better.

"There's no such thing as ghosts," Gerard said, curling his lips.

"C'mon," Stacey prodded. "Every theatre has a ghost. It's tradition."

"Not this theatre," Francesca replied confidently. "Jim has owned and operated it for the past fifteen years and there's not been even the slightest supernatural activity." Stacey opened her mouth to speak, but she quickly interrupted her. "Any strange occurrences you may have witnessed are merely the product of your own imagination."

"Bor-ing," Stacey replied under her breath.

Wendy wouldn't admit it, but she was glad to hear Francesca say that. This theatre was full of dark spaces and strange noises, and she'd much prefer if there wasn't a spirit hanging around, causing trouble.

A string of French curses rang out in the distance and the group moved towards the stage. The director, a short, thin, bald man who was frowning so hard that there were deep creases on his forehead, was standing in the front row of the audience, glaring at them.

"*Que Dieu me vienne en aide*... If I have to ask one more time for actors to take their places..." Jim rumbled. "*Sommes-nous prêts?*"

"English, Jim!" Billy called out. Although he'd said the phrase at least a hundred times today, there was no exasperation in his voice.

Jim frowned and rubbed his temples. "Places for 'Amore.'"

The actors quickly took their places for the top of the scene. Stacey remained in the off-right wing, while Wendy hurried through the cross behind the stage to the off-left wing. Francesca and Gerard moved onstage to the table and chairs Billy had set up after finally hanging the moon to Jim's satisfaction. Once everyone was ready, Jim called for the scene to start.

The sketch was a comment about how the song

"That's Amore" makes no sense and was probably written by someone who was hungry and near an Italian restaurant. Francesca's character was a doe-eyed lover asking Gerard's character to write a romantic love song for her to prove his love. He'd start out fine, but, every time he became stuck, he would look around for inspiration, at which point Wendy or Stacey would cross the stage with some kind of Italian food or drink, which he would add into his song. Francesca would alternate between romantic, confused, and irritated, while Gerard would grow hungrier and more distracted.

Wendy hoisted her first prop, a large cardboard pizza, and prepared for her entrance. As soon as Gerard said her cue line—or, at least, something resembling her cue line—she walked across the stage as if she was delivering the pizza to a couple sitting in the other wing. Stacey gave a nod as Wendy walked past before lifting her own prop, a tray of plastic wine bottles. Her cue came shortly after, and Stacey walked onto the stage, crossing to the other side.

Placing the pizza on the discard table, Wendy looked for her next prop, an imitation of pasta fazool that was quite realistic despite being made of packing peanuts and paint. As she reached for the comically large bowl, she was startled by a sudden loud knocking sound and almost knocked the prop off the table. Shaking it off, she tried to tell herself that it was merely the pipes and it was nothing to worry about, but as soon as she started to relax another knock startled her, this time louder than the first. Taking in a deep breath, she picked up her prop and reminded herself that it was only a mechanical issue. Jim would get someone to check it out soon and then the noise would stop.

Still, as she moved to the wings to listen for her next cue, she couldn't help feeling as if a pair of ghostly eyes were staring at her, watching her hungrily.

CHAPTER TWO

After they finished running through the remainder of the skits, Jim called for the cast and creative to gather in the audience for notes. It took time for everyone to make their way from the various sections of the theatre, but within fifteen minutes the entire troupe had settled into the red, well-worn audience seats.

Wendy had been on her way to sit with Stacey and Carina, but after spying a familiar face she made a detour to the fourth row on the left, where Betty Snow, the props designer, was sitting by herself. Betty was tall and thin, with chin-length red hair that often stuck out in strange directions—usually a result of her nervously playing with it while she worried about a million different things. She was holding a pad of paper and a pencil, ready to take down any notes that Jim might have about the props.

"Nice pasta fazool," Wendy remarked as she neared. "It looked good enough to eat."

Betty smiled and her cheeks flushed at the compliment. "Thanks. It was fun to make. I just hope Jim thinks it's good enough."

Jim, who was standing in front of the stage, chose that

moment to clear his throat loudly. He stared out at the sea of faces before him, a grim look on his face.

Quickly taking a seat, Wendy trained her attention on the short man. She'd thought that the stumble-through had gone pretty well, considering that this was the first time they'd worked with certain props and sets, but the look on Jim's face told her that he didn't feel the same. Not that his expressions had any relation whatsoever to reality—Wendy had been working as an actor for The Quaint Little Theatre for the past six months and had yet to see Jim actually pleased with *anything*. Even if something went well, his expression could only be described as not-angry. It was as if his face was missing the necessary muscles required for smiling.

He quickly launched into his notes about the many things that had bothered him tonight—from the lighting in 'Shakespearean Stories,' to the lack of detail in their current set pieces, to the costume changes not being effective enough in 'Reverse House Party.' Wendy listened carefully as Jim ranted and railed, now familiar enough with this routine to know the difference between general ennui and an actual note. Jim was burdened with memories of grandeur, and most of his comments boiled down to him wanting things to be better but not being able to afford it.

When he reached the end of his list, Jim took a deep breath. "We will start the dress rehearsal tomorrow afternoon at exactly 2:00 pm, and I expect us all to be perfect in preparation for the show tomorrow night. Now go, rest, and be better tomorrow."

Wendy held back a laugh. Inspiring as always...

It had been a long day for the troupe, with the cue-to-cue taking up the morning and afternoon, and then the stumble-through in the evening. Most of them rose wearily to their feet, eager to go home and rest before starting again tomorrow afternoon, but before anyone could leave the room, Francesca stopped them in their tracks.

"Jim, you haven't yet announced which show we'll be doing at the end of the month," she said, her voice projecting loud enough that everyone in the room could hear every word perfectly, no matter where they were standing.

Those who were on their feet quickly sat back down. Although the theatre made most of its money by putting on a variety show twice monthly for a rich benefactor, every month Jim would cast a "legitimate" play for them to rehearse and perform. The variety shows were fun, but the cast and crew enjoyed the chance to work on something serious; something that would exist for more than one night. Their last play had been *Glengarry Glen Ross*, which was an interesting choice for a theatre company that only had six actors—two-thirds of which were women. But with a little script tweaking, Jim had made it work.

Usually, the new play was announced the Monday after the previous show closed, but now it was Wednesday, and Jim still hadn't revealed anything. The cast and crew had spent the past two days wondering if Jim had forgotten to find a new play or if he was withholding the information because he delighted in tormenting them.

Jim grimaced in a way that only a man who constantly had to deal with his ex-wife could. "I am still finalizing *le scénario*. But if you are all so eager to know, I am adapting *Le Fantôme de l'Opéra*." He paused so that they could all murmur excitedly, and once the noise died down a little he continued. "Auditions will be on *Vendredi*, with casting to be announced *juste aprés*."

Although Wendy wasn't fluent in French, she'd picked up enough to understand that auditions would be on Friday and the casting announced shortly after.

Despite Jim's having lived on Jacobi Street for the past fifteen years, he was still reluctant to let go of his native language. Francesca had adapted and now only spoke the odd phrase or two of French, but on certain days it was impossible to convince Jim to speak even a single word of English. It was a sore point for some of the troupe, as most of them didn't speak French, but Wendy was thankful for it. Her heritage was half French and half Inuit, but her parents had wanted to assimilate into their very-white, very-American neighbourhood and refused to speak any language other than English. Wendy's paternal grandparents had died before she was born, and every bit of French she picked up from Jim and Francesca made her feel closer to them.

Now that his announcement was complete, Jim gave a heavy sigh and walked away, heading towards his apartment above the theatre.

"Guess I'd better put the props away," Betty said, giving Wendy a small wave goodbye.

As she watched Betty scurry away, Wendy had a feeling that she would spend the next hour or so trying to fix all the problems Jim had pointed out. While everyone recognized Jim's flair for the dramatic, Betty took most of Jim's notes to heart. She worried about a lot of things—theatre related and otherwise—and didn't want to risk losing her job over the colour of a prop. Others, like the costume designer, Paloma, would merely address one or two notes and call it a night. Paloma knew that no matter how much Jim railed about imperfections, he didn't have the energy to fire them all and hire a brand-new cast and creative.

Wendy looked over and noticed Stacey and Carina talking animatedly in their seats, so she made her way over to them.

"I can't believe he's doing *Phantom*!" Carina exclaimed.

"I know!" Stacy added eagerly. "It's such a great story. So romantic."

"I wonder how different the book is from the musical," Wendy said, leaning on a nearby seat. "I've only ever seen the movie."

Stacey shrugged the comment off. "Knowing Jim, he'll steal a bunch of stuff from the musical and add it in. The musical's super popular, and all he really cares about is making money, which means keeping the audiences happy."

The three of them continued to talk as they made their way backstage, heading for the large dressing room they shared on the lower floor. They were all wearing their final costumes of the night, which was for the skit 'Vamp-liar High.' It was about a girl who arrives at a new high school and discovers that some of the kids are vampires, but who later learns that they're actually humans who are lying in order to seem cool. Stacey, who was playing the new girl, was wearing jeans and a t-shirt, but Wendy and Carina were dressed as wannabe vampires, with dark clothing cut at weird angles and lots of black eyeliner. Although Wendy didn't have many lines in the skit, she was glad that she at least got to wear an elaborate costume.

As they talked about the upcoming auditions, they were very careful not to mention how much each of them wanted the part of Christine. They all knew that only one of them could get the part, and although they secretly hoped the others would fail, nobody would admit it out loud.

Wendy wanted to play Christine more than anything else, but as the newest member of the troupe she wasn't sure if she'd "earned" a role like that yet. Stacey had been working at the theatre for three years, and Carina for two and a half, so the role of the young ingenue in every play went to one of them. Meanwhile, Wendy rarely managed to get a lead role in one of the eight to ten skits they performed every second Thursday. She couldn't help feeling self-conscious sometimes, with Carina's carefree spirit, bronze skin, and long legs; and Stacey's theatrical background off-Broadway, million-dollar smile, and ability to act any part put in front of her. Often Wendy wondered what she brought to this troupe other than her ability to be another body in the background.

Still, it didn't stop her from wanting the part of Christine so bad that she could almost taste it.

"Who do you think is going to play Raoul?" Carina wondered aloud as the group entered the dressing room. It had been built for four people, so it didn't feel cramped when the three of them were inside at the same time, bustling around. There was a long counter along one wall with four mirrors above it, each one lined in large light bulbs that heated the room to an uncomfortable degree if they were left on for too long. Along the other wall were four closets where they could each hang up their clothes and costumes, and store personal items. There was also a shower and bathroom at one end, opposite the entrance. Next door was another dressing room exactly like it, which had been assigned to Gerard and Sam. There were four private dressing rooms on the main floor, behind the stage, but those were reserved for people with lead roles or who had been named Francesca.

"We can all agree that it won't be Samuel, right?" Stacey burst out laughing. "I mean, he's old enough to be our grandfather."

"Maybe it'll be Gerard," Carina suggested as she wiped the heavy make-up from her face.

Wendy and Stacey exchanged a look. Although Gerard was younger than Samuel and looked younger than his fifty years of age, neither of them wanted to play his love interest. They knew that Carina, however, wouldn't have any qualms about that.

"I don't know," Stacey said as she quickly changed into her regular clothes, "I mean, during *A Streetcar Named Desire* he kept changing up his blocking and lines, and I never felt like I knew where I was."

"That's just his process," Carina replied diplomatically.

"Well, I wish he'd get another one," Stacey muttered.

Wendy held back a laugh. "Do you think Jim might try to get Billy to do it?" Although Billy had enough to do with designing the sets and lighting, he had no problem stepping in for a bit part occasionally. While he'd never expressed a desire for a bigger part, she'd feel more comfortable with him in the role instead of Gerard, even if he was nearly fifteen years her senior.

"Or Scott?" Stacey pretended to gag. "That would be the worst."

Carina wrinkled her nose. "I bet he'd do it if Jim promised him the chance to finally assistant direct something."

"Maybe one of us will end up playing it," Wendy interjected, quickly changing the subject. Although she didn't like the way that Scott skulked around the theatre, acting as if he owned it (or *should* own it), she didn't want to say anything that he might hear. It was well known that he had a habit of listening at closed doors, and while some people didn't care one bit about what he might think, she didn't want to make enemies of anyone at the theatre. "I mean, we've certainly played enough male roles in the past. Besides, Raoul and Christine are supposed to be childhood friends and we're closer in age than any of the men."

"Well, let's just hope that Jim isn't planning on casting Francesca as Christine," Stacey said bitterly. "I wouldn't be surprised if she demanded to play the part."

"Oh, that would be the worst!" Carina cried, slumping against the counter. "I mean, losing that part would be terrible, but it'd be even worse if it was to *her*."

Wendy finished hanging up her costume and picked up her purse. She hadn't managed to get all her eyeliner off, but the gossip was starting to overwhelm her. "See you two tomorrow afternoon," she said as she stepped into the hallway.

She could hear noises farther down the hall as designers cleaned up their workspaces or discussed Jim's notes with each other or adjusted certain projects. A smile broke out on her face as she thought about how lucky she was to work in a place that was so full of life, where people truly enjoyed what they did.

As Wendy made her way to the staircase, she kept an ear out for the strange noise that she'd heard earlier in the wings. At first it seemed as if the noise had gone away, but, as she started to ascend the staircase, she heard a sharp knock and instinctively looked towards the door to the basement.

It was a perfectly normal door, located next to the staircase, leading to a large room that housed the furnace, and which they also used to store backdrops and furniture. She'd walked past it hundreds of times, but, as she looked at it now, it took on a sinister quality. The dark red paint seemed redder and more chipped, with jagged pieces sticking out and flaking off, like dried blood. As she continued to stare at the door, a sudden, ear-splitting knock from within rattled the door and caused her to jump. She quickly hurried up the stairs, her heart pounding in her chest.

CHAPTER THREE

Stepping outside The Quaint Little Theatre, Wendy took in a deep breath of the cool night air. Now that she was away from the basement door, she felt a lot better. Shaking her head, she chided herself for being so easy to scare. It was probably one of the other actors playing a joke.

As she took in her surroundings, she saw that even though it was late evening, the street was alive with people heading to and from the many businesses that occupied Jacobi Street. Despite the short length of the street, it was packed full of vendors, markets, galleries, and theatres, with plenty of apartments tucked around. Most of the people who worked on the street lived here, creating a harmonious, symbiotic feeling within the neighbourhood. That magical feeling was likely helped by the fact that the street rarely existed on any maps, making it more difficult for ordinary folk to find. This street belonged to the people who lived on it, and they all knew it.

A smile crossed Wendy's face as she thought of how lucky she'd been to discover it.

She had grown up further north in the city, completely oblivious of Jacobi Street and its charming ways. Although she'd dabbled in high school drama, Wendy had never once considered becoming an actor. Her parents had always wanted her to go to college and become an accountant like her mother or a data analyst like her father, but neither option sounded ideal. In fact, the whole notion of college was unappealing to her. So, despite her parents' objections, Wendy decided not to go. She found a full-time job working at one of the restaurants downtown, and once she'd earned enough money she moved out of her parents' home and away from their expectations. Deciding that life was good enough for now, she spent three years working at the restaurant, enjoying her freedom from her parents' rules and assumptions.

It wasn't until she noticed a paper sign taped to a light pole on 13th Street that the course of her life changed dramatically. The sign was eye-catching in its simplicity, with hand-drawn curtains and a stage framing the notice. All the other signs had been printed on glossy paper and looked professionally designed, so this one stood out like a sore thumb. The name of the theatre sounded vaguely familiar, although she'd never been to it, and the sign said that it was looking for an actor for its bi-weekly variety show.

At that moment, she began to wonder what it would be like to be an actor. The plays she'd been in during high school had been fun, and although she suspected that this would be a lot more work, it had to be better than occasionally getting yelled at for the soup not being warm enough or for getting an order wrong—even though it was exactly how the customer had ordered it. After an hour of debat-

ing the matter with herself, she decided to try out and see
what happened. If she got in then perhaps she'd give acting a try, and if she failed horribly then she'd still have the
restaurant to go back to.

Finding Jacobi Street hadn't been easy, but after a few
false starts Wendy finally discovered the entrance off 14th
Street. She must have walked past it many times over the
last few years, but never once noticed where it led. On
the day of the auditions, she stepped onto the cobblestone
street for the first time, keeping an eye out for The Quaint
Little Theatre, but also getting distracted by this strange,
wondrous street that she had never known existed. There
were no cars, and it was crammed full of tall, thin houses
that had been converted into businesses. Everyone seemed
to know everyone else. For a minute she wondered if she
had suddenly started hallucinating. No other street in the
city looked or felt like this.

When she found the theatre and stepped inside, she
was surprised that such a luxurious place could exist in
such an unassuming building. The long hallway she found
herself in was carpeted and ran the length of the building,
with another door at the end, likely leading back to 14th
Street. There appeared to be a small Box Office window
further down on her right, and on her left were two large
wooden doors that were propped open. They led into the
auditorium, which was even more surprising. The room
was huge, easily able to seat 200 people, and the style was
baroque, with elaborate wall-fixtures and a gilded frame
around the raised proscenium stage. The theatre had definitely seen better days, but it was still grander than any
other theatre that Wendy had been to. There were large

red curtains framing either side of the stage, and the orchestra was filled with fold-down chairs in a similar red.

An older, bald man with a round head was talking to a large blonde woman and a larger man with brown hair and a bushy brown beard near the stage. She wondered if they were also auditioning or if they worked here. There hadn't been any number to phone and ask questions, so Wendy had decided to show up and hope for the best. However, she could feel uncertainty growing inside of her as she walked further into the auditorium, passing by row after row of red chairs. This theatre looked way more professional than she'd been expecting, and now she was worried that she was completely out of her league. Coming to a stop, Wendy wondered if she should continue to the stage or turn around and go back home before anyone noticed her arrival.

Before she could decide, the group realized that a newcomer was in their midst and all eyes turned towards her.

"Hi...?" she called out nervously. "I'm here to audition..."

"*Venez ici*," the bald man said, waving her forward.

Wendy wasn't sure what the man had said or which language he'd spoken, but she assumed that he meant for her to come closer. With a ton of butterflies fluttering in her stomach, she walked towards the group of three, and what commenced was the strangest experience she'd ever had.

Although she'd come prepared with a monologue, she had no idea that she needed a professional head-shot or resume (nor had that information been included on the poster). As she tried to remember the few plays she'd been in during high school, she could see the French man becoming more and more impatient, and she began to regret her impulsiveness. She fumbled the beginning of her monologue but managed to push through and finish stronger, and when they asked her to sing, her mind blanked for a few seconds before she hastily brought out a pop song she'd last sung in the shower that morning. The other man and woman, who had introduced themselves as Billy and Francesca, tried to keep the mood friendly and light, but they weren't entirely able to combat Jim's obvious hostility.

When Wendy left the theatre, she was certain that she'd never be able to show her face on this street ever again, which was a bit of a shame. She'd love to go back but wouldn't want to risk the chance of running into the angry director again. He seemed like the type that would hold a grudge. However, the very next day she received a call from Francesca saying that if she wanted to become a part of their troupe, they would hire her. Then Francesca told her what kind of work the theatre did, what would be expected of her, and named a price that was less than she was earning at the restaurant, but still seemed ridiculously high for an actor in a bi-weekly variety show. Although Wendy suspected that she was being hired because she was the only person who'd auditioned—and she was still a little afraid of Jim—she also knew that she really wanted the job.

And thus she became the newest troupe member of The Quaint Little Theatre. Mostly she worked background and bit parts, learning what was involved in putting on a show, and eventually she began to grow and get better. After her first month with the troupe, she moved into a small studio flat above the Oz Theatre, an old movie house that only showed Technicolour movies—except on April Fool's Day when they'd play black and white movies.

Since then, the rest of the world began to fall away. Her relationship with her parents, which was tense due to her unwillingness to follow their plans, became further strained by her new career path. The friends she'd made at the restaurant didn't understand why she would quit a well-paying job to work in a theatre and earn less, and they had no desire to even look for Jacobi Street, let alone watch her perform. But Wendy didn't care. She found new friends within the troupe and a new life that challenged and excited her. The more time she spent on Jacobi Street, the more convinced she became that this was where she was meant to be.

CHAPTER FOUR

"You did wonderful work tonight, darling," Francesca said, coming up beside Wendy and pulling her from her thoughts. "You've come a long way in the past few months."

She paused expectantly and Wendy knew exactly what she wanted to hear.

"It's all thanks to you," Wendy replied. It was something she would have said anyway, but Francesca didn't like to rely on chance whenever a compliment was involved.

A little over a month after Wendy had joined the troupe, Francesca decided to take her under her wing and provide acting and singing lessons—something she'd never offered to anyone else. Although *la grande dame du théâtre* was intimidating as hell, Wendy was cognizant enough to realize that she desperately needed the help if she ever wanted to be considered an asset to the team. The best part was that Francesca didn't ask for money, she merely asked for an opportunity to share the wealth of knowledge she'd amassed over many years as a professional actor in Paris. And—although Wendy would never admit it out loud—she was sure that Francesca did it because it gave her the chance to revisit her heyday and wistfully reminisce about all the wonderful parts she'd played in the past.

"Now, darling, tell me that you've been keeping up with your practice," Francesca said as they walked away from the theatre. She rented the one-bedroom apartment on the floor below Wendy, so they sometimes walked home together. In fact, Francesca had been the one to suggest to Wendy that she should move onto the street and let her know that the apartment upstairs needed a tenant.

"I have," Wendy replied, being careful to make her pace slower to match the older woman's.

"Good, because the part of Christine is basically yours if you want it."

Wendy stopped in her tracks, her eyes widening in surprise. "Really?"

"Of course, darling," Francesca said, sounding as if she was stating a fact that everyone knew. She paused and turned to Wendy, regarding her fondly. "With all the training I've been giving you, you've become quite the star in hiding. All you need is the perfect audition to show Jim just how talented you are. Give me a few hours and I will find you the perfect piece. Trust me, Wendy. After all, I played Christine in *Les Joueurs de Paris*' performance of *The Phantom of the Opera* musical by Andrew Lloyd Webber, so I know exactly what's required."

"I guess that means you want to play Carlotta?" she said carefully.

Francesca laughed. "Of course. Carlotta has a much more expressive role and lends itself to more humour. I've played so many ingenues, my dear, that these days I crave variety. You'll see once you've gotten more roles under your belt."

As they continued walking, Francesca spoke of her time with *Les Joueurs de Paris*. Every so often she would pause to say hello or wave to someone on the street, but then immediately pick the story back up right where she'd left off. They soon reached the Oz Theatre, which was currently playing *Viennese Nights*, and headed up to their respective apartments.

"Have a good night," Francesca said with a wink, before disappearing into her apartment.

Wendy smiled at the closed door before continuing up the staircase. Because her apartment was on the fourth floor, she basically lived in the attic. The walls went about four feet high before the ceiling sloped inwards on two sides, but the rent was cheap enough that she didn't mind occasionally knocking her head. It was a bachelor apartment, but she'd found some folding screens to place around her bed to give the illusion that there was some kind of separation between the "bedroom" and the "living room." It gave the room a quirky, bohemian quality that fit in with the rest of the buildings on the street, and it made her feel more like an artist.

Walking over to the fridge, she took out a bottle of white wine that had been chilling since the morning. Taking two glasses from the cupboard, she left one on the counter and poured wine into the other. Putting the bottle back in the fridge, she picked up her glass and walked over to the couch, turning on the television.

Her glass was almost empty when there was a knock

on her door.

"It's open," Wendy called out.

"Sorry I'm so late," Betty said as she entered the apartment. She walked over to the couch and greeted Wendy with a kiss. "It took me longer than I thought to get everything ready for tomorrow."

"It's okay," Wendy said. "I know you're a hard worker. There's wine in the fridge if you want."

Betty's smile grew as she moved into the kitchen area. "If I want? When have you ever known me not to want wine?"

"Better top me up while you're at it."

Once the wine was poured and snacks were retrieved, they settled on the couch together. Wendy sat at one end while Betty curled up next to her, leaning her head on her shoulder. They settled on a channel playing *The Princess Bride*, which they'd already seen a hundred times but still loved watching.

"Oh," Betty said suddenly, sitting up straight and turning to Wendy. "On my way up here, Francesca stopped me and told me to tell you..." she paused and screwed up her face as she struggled to remember. "Mina after she drinks Dracula's blood in... Dietz's *Dracula,* and Christine's song from the *Phantom* musical."

Wendy paused for thought before nodding. "That makes sense."

Betty reached for some chips. "Do you want to explain what that means? Or would you rather I spend an hour guessing?"

"Francesca's helping me choose a good monologue for the *Phantom* auditions. I guess since Christine's a singer it'll be smart to have a song ready."

Betty nodded approvingly. "I still can't believe she hasn't said anything to anyone about us yet. I keep expecting her to shout it from the rooftops."

Wendy smiled. "Turns out, Francesca knows how to keep a secret."

Wendy and Betty had been secretly dating for two months, although they'd been secretly flirting for longer. Neither was sure how the other actually felt until late one night, after an incredibly inebriated cast party, when the two had managed to sneak away from everyone else and get some things straight—or, actually, not-so-straight.

Betty took in a deep breath. "I almost told Galia yesterday."

Wendy sat up straighter and gave her an encouraging smile. She knew that Betty desperately wanted to tell her sister about the two of them but was too scared. Their parents had been extremely conservative and had a lot of strict rules and racist opinions, which is why the sisters decided to move out of the house after both of them finished high school. They ended up on Jacobi Street, almost as if by providence, and had jobs at the theatre within two weeks. Even though it was only the two of them in their small apartment above Pangea Market, Betty said that it felt more like home than their parents' house ever had.

Wendy suspected that Galia would be okay with the news that her little sister was dating someone of the same gender, but Betty wasn't sure enough to say anything. She didn't want to risk her sister freaking out and kicking her out of the apartment they shared or refusing to talk to her. She didn't want to lose the only family she had left.

Although Wendy didn't have any strong familial connections, she knew what it was like to hide a part of her true self. She had never come out as bisexual to her parents, figuring that it would disappoint them as much as her lack of college ambition or—even worse—that they'd think it was a phase she'd grow out of once she met the right man. Though she wanted to be able to hold hands in public and cuddle up together at the theatre, she would never push Betty to do anything she didn't feel comfortable doing.

"We were having supper last night and Galia remarked that I'd been spending more time with my 'paramour,'" Betty said, filling Wendy in. "She said that she knew our place was small, but it'd be okay with her if the two of us spent time here, at the apartment. I almost told her right then and there, but she said something else." Betty paused, a pained look crossing her face. "She said, she'd love to meet *him*."

Wendy put her arm around Betty and pulled her close. "It's okay," she said softly.

"I'm sorry, Wendy. I don't want to keep you a secret, but..."

"It's okay," she repeated. "It's okay."

They sat together in silence for a while, the movie playing in the background, Wendy's arms wrapped protectively around Betty. At least in this apartment they didn't have to hide.

"You know, you did good in rehearsal tonight," Betty said, changing the subject to something lighter. "Jim really should give you better parts."

"Well, other than Carina, I've been there the shortest

amount of time."

"Yeah, but I'd put talent above time served."

"I don't think the other girls would see it that way," Wendy remarked, reaching for her glass.

Betty scoffed. "If Stacey doesn't like it then she can go straight back to off-Broadway, like she keeps threatening to do. She's good in some parts, I'll give her that, but she's not that great at playing vulnerable. And Carina thinks that fucking Gerard is the best way to get better parts, but she's actually not that versatile of an actor. She needs to spend more time on her script and less time on Gerard's dick."

Wendy considered those observations. "I won't agree with you, but I also won't argue."

A wide smile broke out on Betty's face. "Because you know I'm right!"

"I think the wine is making you smarter," Wendy laughed.

"Then I'd better get some more," Betty said before tipping her glass back and finishing off the contents.

Wendy joined her, quickly finishing off what was left in her own glass. As she reached for Betty's to get a refill, Betty leaned in for a kiss, and soon all thoughts of wine were pushed aside.

CHAPTER FIVE

Scott held his clipboard close to his chest as he stepped through the basement door. The light from the furnace gave the room a red glow that seemed to signify that you were about to descend into hell. He turned on the light switch near the door, but only half of the large bulbs in the ceiling lit up. He wondered if Billy knew about this or if it was another one of Jim's cost-saving measures.

As he made his way down the metal stairs, the steps clanging and shaking slightly under his feet, Scott could feel animosity rising up within him. Jim didn't care one bit about the strange noises the furnace was making, but the matter had been brought up by Francesca, and he knew that she'd never give him a moment's peace until it was resolved. This led to Jim barking at Scott to go check out the furnace after rehearsal, and when Scott mentioned that he knew nothing about furnaces, Jim let out a string of curses that only ended when Scott agreed to go and take a look.

It was difficult not to feel sour. He knew that the only reason he had a job at this theatre was because his uncle was the theatre's benefactor and had pulled some strings, but he'd always hoped that eventually Jim would give him a chance to prove that he could be valuable. Unfortunately, Jim only saw him as an extra body, available for all the jobs nobody else wanted to do. This was a perfect example—Billy would be a much better choice for checking out whether a furnace was okay or not, but Jim didn't care enough to send the best person for the job. He simply wanted to give the impression that he was doing something about it.

Some days, Scott wondered if he should ask his uncle to step in and make Jim give him a better position. When he'd learned about his uncle's activities, Scott decided that it would be great if he could become a director. Of course, he didn't expect to start directing shows straight out of the gate, but he'd been hoping that Jim would let him be an assistant director and show him the ropes. Instead, he became the person who fetched coffee and set up tables and got shoved into an ill-fitting costume whenever they needed a silent body on stage. It would be easy enough for him to make the suggestion, but he didn't want his uncle to have to step in. He wanted to prove that he didn't need someone else to solve his problems—he could solve them on his own.

As Scott stepped off the staircase, he took a deep breath and walked towards the back of the room, where the furnace was located. There was something about the low, intermittent knocking sound coming from the back of the room that unsettled him. He looked around, but nobody else seemed to be down here. There was nothing but stacked backdrops and set pieces on either side, leaving a crude hallway in the centre of the room which led to the back, where the furnace angrily glowed red. Scott had been ordered down here many times to fetch items, but he'd never gone as far back as the furnace and he wished that it could remain that way. Maybe he could lie and tell Jim that he'd taken a look and nothing was wrong. No, that wouldn't be smart. If something went wrong later then he'd be to blame, and if Jim found out that he hadn't taken this request seriously, it could hurt his future in the company.

A particularly loud knock almost made him drop the clipboard. Tightening his grip on it, he slowly walked forward. Another noise startled him, but it wasn't a knock this time, it was a low scraping sound. Scott paused. He'd been told that a furnace could make knocking sounds if air or an animal was trapped in the pipes, but what could make a scraping noise? Was there any part of a furnace that could scrape? Had something come loose?

He took a tentative step forward. The horrible scraping sound grew louder. It was like something sharp was being dragged along metal, and it almost sounded as if it was moving towards him.

"Hello?" Scott called out. "Is anyone back there?"

He tried to remember who had been upstairs when Jim sent him down here. He wouldn't put it past anyone in the troupe to hide down here and scare him. Some of them enjoyed playing tricks on him, like the time someone stole his clipboard and put it in Jell-O.

Summoning up all his courage, Scott moved forward.

"I know you're down here, so there's no point trying to scare me."

Another scrape made him jump, but at least he didn't

cry out in fear.

"You might as well show yourself," he continued, putting as much false confidence into his voice as he could muster.

Scott continued towards the furnace, preparing himself for the jump scare that would come. However, nothing could have prepared him for the large shape that stepped out of the shadows and moved his way.

His clipboard fell to the ground as a terrified shriek escaped his lips.

CHAPTER SIX

Backstage at the theatre, the energy was almost too much for the building to contain. Designers were rushing around, making sure that the props and costumes had been placed correctly, that the set pieces were all in order, and that everything was ready for tonight's show. Some actors paced the hallways as they went over lines, while others were meticulously following pre-show rituals in the hopes that it would make tonight perfect (or at least minimize the number of mistakes that could happen).

All throughout the chaos was Ari, the stage manager, who was calmly going through their final checks while actors randomly approached to ask them questions about cues, and entrances and exits, and other information which had been forgotten due to pre-show nerves.

Wendy tried to keep out of the way as much as possible while doing her pre-show checks. Some people would have no qualms about running her over if she got in their way for even a second. The desperate need to have everything perfect for the show seemed to make people more frantic and self-obsessed than normal. Well, other than Scott, who seemed to be doing his best to avoid everyone else. Normally he'd at least try to project a bit of authority and give someone a pointless order, but tonight he seemed to have given in to the fact that he had no real power, except for the tiny bit that Jim allowed him.

Turning her attention away from everyone else, Wendy continued her pre-show ritual, which involved going through her script one last time before making sure all her props and costumes were in their correct places. There were five sketches before intermission and five afterwards, so it was a lot to keep track of, even if she wasn't in every sketch. At least this time she only had two quick-changes that she'd have to do in the wings. There was enough time between her other costume changes for her to go down to the dressing room and get ready in a less hectic mode.

There were a few sketches that were one or two people, but most sketches involved four to six actors, so everyone had lots to do during the show. Jim made sure to pace the larger skits with the smaller, to give some people a chance to catch their breath, and had even created some skits, like Billy's "Stagehand Shuffle," to give the actors time to gear up for a bigger sketch. Everything was carefully planned so that the cast and crew could move easily and effectively from one sketch to the next—barring any kind of unexpected disaster.

Wendy used to wonder why they bothered being be so elaborate with the show and the sets, especially since they were only sketches and only existed for one night, but then someone informed her that if it wasn't for the money that J.P. Lodge shelled out for these shows, the theatre wouldn't be able to hire half as many people or produce any other works.

After confirming that her props and costumes were properly set, Wendy walked over to the curtain and peeked outside. There were about 30 people in the audience, which was good, all things considered. In the beginning the variety show had been attended only by Mr. Lodge and a few of his friends, but then Mr. Lodge began inviting more friends, and then the residents of Jacobi Street began attending and it became something like a community gathering. That was the way of the street—those who lived here supported the local businesses whenever possible.

The past few months had been hard on the street, with several disappearances that still remained unsolved. Some suspected that the people had simply run away, likely due to embezzlement (the owner of The Menagerie gallery) or affairs (Mr. Cooper, of Cooper's General Market) or getting into serious trouble that they needed to disappear from (one of the local street artists, Obi). Although the reasons were sound, others weren't so sure. It would have been strange enough for one person to disappear without a word, but for so many to go within a couple weeks... Whatever the reasons, it was difficult for many residents to accept. There weren't a lot of people who lived on the street and they were all quite familiar with one another, so it was a shock for someone to just up and leave without notice, even if it wasn't entirely out of the realm of possibility.

Tonight's audience seemed like they were in a good mood and ready to laugh, which helped calm Wendy a little. She always felt nervous before a show, no matter how prepared she was. It was the thrill of live theatre, where anything could happen—and often did. Someone might bring on the wrong prop, say the wrong line, or wear the wrong costume. The joy of the variety show was that there was always a way to pretend that a mistake was a part of the act, even when it wasn't.

Stepping away from the curtains, she headed back to the dressing room to get into her first costume.

Jim settled into his seat near the back of the theatre, a frown on his face and his arms crossed over his chest. During rehearsals he sat closer to the stage, to get a better idea of how the show was going, but whenever there was an audience in the house he wanted to sit as far away as possible to try to avoid recognition. Not that his choice of seating mattered, since everyone in attendance knew that he was the writer and director, but over time the patrons had learned to think of him as an eccentric creative and give him some space. A few still waved hello to him, but they all refrained from trying to start discussions.

A few minutes later, Scott came out from backstage and hurried over to a chair that was near the back and on the opposite side of the theatre, nowhere close to Jim. Jim frowned as he thought about the annoying young man with the coke-bottle glasses. As much as Scott wanted to be a director, Jim knew that he was all wrong for the part. Sure, he sometimes had "ideas," but he had no concept of the "big picture." Whenever Jim mentioned it to him, Scott would narrow his eyes and act as if such a thing wasn't important.

Scott also had no authority whatsoever and let the actors and designers run all over him, which would only lead to chaos in rehearsals. Jim had a feeling that the kid had never been involved in theatre before being hired here, and had simply woken up one day, realized that his uncle was patron to a theatre, and decided to jump in head first. If it weren't for Lodge's patronage, Jim never would have considered hiring the slimy young man, but Lodge was thankful for Jim's giving his nephew something to do and actually gave more money to the theatre because of it. So, although Scott was a twerp, he at least had *some* value.

As Jim looked up at the red velvet curtains that currently hid the stage from view, he could almost imagine that he was back in Paris, waiting for the premiere of one of his plays. It had been so much easier back then, to bask in the glory of the applause and recognition. Back then he'd created *art*, and people had been more than willing to throw money at him, eager to contribute to such an honoured and highly esteemed craft. In those days, if you'd asked what he thought the future would be like, he never would have entertained the idea that he'd end up in some strange American city, desperately pinching pennies, and performing ridiculous sketches for people who'd never been in a theatre larger than two hundred seats.

Perhaps he'd been too proud in his earlier life, but since then he'd had more than enough humility for nine hundred lives. How he wished that he could snap his fingers and be back in Paris, among the opulent theatres where the red curtains were soft and not worn bare in places, where the gold accents were shiny and untarnished, where the ropes always worked and the joists were well-oiled, and where whatever he wanted was within his grasp.

Nowadays, it was the small things that kept him going. Soon he'd put the finishing touches on his script for *Le Fantôme* and show this street how real theatre was done. He'd wanted to perform this show for ages, but there hadn't been enough money to do it properly. Over the past few years, he'd scrimped and saved in order to bring this show to life in a way that did it justice. He'd show everyone what the theatres of Paris were like, and how terrifying and breath-taking a theatrical experience could be.

The door next to the stage opened and Rhonda entered the auditorium, walking over to the upright piano beside the stage. Jim was pleased to see that she was wearing a long-sleeved black dress with no embellishments. For the first few shows after she was hired, she'd worn bright and colourful clothing, assuming that it would be appropriate for a show like this, and Jim had to inform her that the audience was here to look at the stage and not her. She caught on quickly, and although she'd successfully argued for the right to wear costumes during any "themed" variety shows they put on—like Halloween and Valentine's Day—she at least gave him less of a headache than most of the other crew.

Rhonda sat in front of the piano and began to play the introduction music for the show. Taking a deep breath, Jim steadied himself as the curtain rose.

First up was Samuel, whose job it was to welcome the patrons. Jim had hired him because he fit the image of a typical paternal character, and it was always handy to have someone like that around. Samuel had worked in professional theatre for a long time, until the roles started drying up. Jim suspected that it was because Samuel considered himself the greatest actor to have ever lived—a notion that grew old quite fast. In Paris, Jim would have kicked him to the street, but here he had to take what he could get. Samuel was useful as the show's greeter, as he lent gravitas to the introduction and provided a proxy in which Mr. Lodge and his friends could see themselves and imagine what it would be like to be on stage.

After a few words, Samuel introduced the first sketch, and as he left the stage the curtains opened, revealing a restaurant set with a small table and two chairs. The skit was about two people who were in love, except one person was a vampire and the other wouldn't give up garlic. As Jim watched Gerard and Stacey perform the skit, he observed that Stacey had indeed taken the note he'd given her about exaggerating her expressions more. He also noticed that Carina, who was playing their waitress, had hiked her skirt up a couple extra inches, and that Gerard was constantly sneaking glances her way, despite his character's love for the vampire seated across from him. The skit ended with Gerard swearing that his love for Stacey was the most important thing in the world, and that he would give up garlic forever to be with her, but as soon as she'd left the stage, he ordered a large plate of garlic bread. Holding the bread close, he swore that he'd give up garlic tomorrow before pretending to dive in. The audience clapped and a black curtain descended, covering up the back half of the stage and the set, giving the illusion that the stage was empty.

The lighting changed to something more joyful, and Francesca walked onstage wearing a shimmering blue and white dress with a short skirt. She began to sing "Anything Goes" from the Broadway musical of the same name, engaging the audience with her energy and character. While she sang, a smile crossed Jim's face, and for a moment he fell in love with her all over again. As she enchanted the crowd with her voice and talent, he was able to see the young woman he'd married those many years ago. But all too soon the song ended, and she disappeared offstage, and the reality of his life came rushing back.

The black curtain flew up, revealing a skit about two co-workers finding a birthday cake in the break room and not knowing whose birthday it was. It starred Wendy and Carina, who ended up realizing that they knew absolutely nothing about their co-workers, including most of their names. Eventually they decided to go and pretend that they hadn't seen the cake, but before they could leave, Samuel's character walked in and started asking questions. The two of them convinced Samuel's character that it was a surprise for him, and that the name on the cake being someone else's was part of that surprise, before quickly running away and ending the scene.

The black curtain dropped again. After another lighting change, Francesca walked onstage wearing an elaborate Elizabethan outfit and began to retell "Goodnight Moon" in the Shakespearean tongue. Other actors, dressed all in black, moved props across the stage, animating the story.

The final skit before intermission was 'Mad House Party,' which was about two college kids and their desire to throw a rager of a party. Although it started out crazy, as more people showed up, the party became tamer and tamer, until it finally turned into a Victorian tea party— much to the chagrin of the hosts.

As the curtain came down and the audience applauded, Jim breathed a small sigh of relief. The first half of the show had passed without any major issues and the audience seemed to have enjoyed it. There was still the second half to get through, but it looked like the troupe was having a good night. Then again, he knew better than to assume everything would be okay. Some people relaxed when a show was going well, which often led to mistakes.

When the lights to the auditorium came on, most of the audience headed out to The Orchestra Pit, the bar next door. It was the smallest bar on Jacobi Street, and was run by a Scandinavian man who spoke with an extremely thick accent that was difficult to understand most of the time. The man attended all their shows, and during intermission he would turn his living room into a bar, providing a limited assortment of alcoholic and non-alcoholic drinks to patrons, along with some snacks. Jim had to hand it to him—the man had noticed an opportunity and seized it.

As much as Jim wanted a drink right now, he didn't want to stand in line with the common public; shoulder to shoulder with someone who'd likely offer him a "brilliant" idea for the next show. He briefly toyed with the idea of going upstairs and pouring a drink from his personal bar, but he had an odd feeling that if he took his eyes off the stage something terrible would happen. Instead, he stayed in his seat and waited for the minutes to pass.

Finally, everyone arrived back in the auditorium and it was time for the second half of the show to begin. It started with a skit of two reviewers talking about the show so far, giving a humorous review of the first act's skits. As it played, Jim glared at the back of Walter Astoria's head, hoping that the reviewer for the local paper would be able to see that 1) the troupe could take a joke and 2) reviewers were ridiculous. It was something Jim absolutely hated about this city: the fact that there was only one theatre reviewer who came to this theatre, and that he was a terrible, twisted man who couldn't understand the value of variety shows. Astoria seemed to think that *all* theatre needed to be some grand fantastic message, so while he was sometimes fond of their actual shows, he constantly eviscerated the variety show. Thankfully, Mr. Lodge didn't care about reviews—all he wanted was to be entertained.

Next was a skit about Benvolio and Balthasar from *Romeo and Juliet* falling in love behind the scenes of the play as tragedy ensued around them. It quickly moved into the 'Amore' sketch, after which the black curtain descended, and Billy came onstage to tell jokes and charm the audience while everyone else set up the scene for the final skit. The 'Stagehand Shuffle' had started out as Billy buying time to cover up an incident backstage that slowed the set-up of the next scene, but it turned out that audiences liked Billy so much that Jim had to make it a regular part of the show. The jokes Billy told were rarely funny, but he had an endearing warmth that people liked.

The 'Shuffle' went well, as it always did, and then it was time for 'Vamp-liar High.' The skit commented on a lot of current pop-culture trends and made fun of tired, old franchises, and the audience absolutely ate it up.

Finally, the actors took their bows and the curtain closed for the final time that night. Jim took in a deep breath and affixed a smile to his face. First, he'd talk to Mr. Lodge about the show, and maybe a few other audience members, but then he'd be able to retire to his apartment and continue working on a script that actually mattered to him.

CHAPTER SEVEN

There was something about applause that brought a wide smile to Wendy's face. After all the hard work they'd done putting the show together, it was nice to know that their audience had enjoyed and appreciated it. Sure, it seemed like a silly little show full of sketches and jokes, but it made people laugh and forget about their troubles for a while, and that made it worth all the trouble.

The red velvet curtains closed, and the actors made their way offstage. The wings, which had started the night meticulously organized, were now a mess. Props had been thrown in and around discard boxes, costumes were hanging over every available surface, and set pieces had been shoved any place that they could fit. Despite the discord, there was a jubilant feeling amongst the entire troupe. The show hadn't been entirely perfect, but they'd gotten through it and the audience was none the wiser.

As the actors made their way to their dressing rooms to change, the designers started clearing up, gathering the items from their departments quickly and efficiently. Now that the show was over, it was time for everyone's favourite part of the night—the cast party. The faster everything was put away, the sooner they could start celebrating a successful show.

"Did you see how I almost dropped that pizza?" Stacey said as she tossed her costume into the laundry hamper Paloma had placed in their room earlier. "I mean, I thought it was going to fly out of my hands and brain that guy in the first row. He'd have deserved it for sitting in the front row, but still..."

"At least you didn't drop a book on Francesca's foot," Carina countered, shimming into a tight red dress. "I thought she was going to kill me after the house party sketch."

"She still might," Stacey warned. "Better watch out or she'll push you from the top of The Treehouse!" Stacey waved her fingers in Carina's direction and made spooky noises.

Wendy held back her laughter and tried to keep a straight face as she straightened the neckline of her dark blue sweater dress.

Carina scoffed and tossed her hair to the side. "I'm sure I could take her in a fight. Zip me up?"

Wendy walked over and zipped Carina into her dress. "I'd stay away from any windows, nevertheless," she warned playfully.

"Hey, if you die," Stacey said, abruptly turning away from her make-up routine, "can you come back and haunt the theatre? I still can't believe we don't have a ghost. I mean, *every* theatre has a ghost. It's so lame."

Carina rolled her eyes. "When I die, which will be a long time from now, I hope that I'll get to rest in peace. Although, if it happens that one of the actors here kills me, I might see about sticking around for a day or so to torment them."

Smiling, Stacey gave her plan two thumbs up before returning to her lipstick application.

When they were finished, the three of them exited the dressing room, eager to party. Wendy glanced down the hall, where the costume, special effects, props, and carpentry rooms were located. She knew that it would take Betty a while to get to the bar since she had to put away all the props that were used tonight—and there had been a *lot* of props. Since the two of them weren't "official," she had no valid reason to stay behind and help Betty, and so she continued walking with Stacey and Carina.

When they headed up the stairs, Wendy couldn't help glancing at the basement door, which looked exactly the same as it had last week. There had been no strange knocking tonight, which relieved her. Hopefully, the furnace problem had been solved.

"I still can't believe that a person genuinely laughed at Billy's joke about the hedgehogs," Carina remarked as they made their way into the street.

"Did they? I couldn't hear anything over the groans," Wendy said.

Stacey smiled widely. "I have it on good authority that the guy who laughed might be Billy's current paramour."

Carina gasped in mock horror. "You mean there's two men out there who have a sense of humour like that? How terrible!"

"At least they've found each other and are sparing the rest of us," Stacey pointed out, to which the others had to agree.

They quickly reached The Treehouse, but that was the way of Jacobi Street—no matter where a person started, it never took long to reach their destination. The building was three-stories tall, with the first floor set up as an art gallery devoted to the owner's father's artwork. The main bar was on the second floor, and there was a private room on the third, where people could go to get away from the crowds or rent for parties. The troupe had a great relationship with Calie, who owned the building and lived in the basement, and Calie would always hold the third floor for them after each show. Wendy suspected that Calie did this because she knew they'd spend an obscene amount of money on alcohol and snacks.

The gallery was closed this late at night; not that any of them would have suggested skipping the party to go inside. Wendy sometimes thought about going in and checking out the artwork, but often it was a fleeting thought she had while on her way to the bar. Calie worked both businesses, so when the bar was open, the gallery was closed, and vice versa.

Climbing up to the second floor, the group headed over to the bar, which was a semi-circle set against one of the walls. Behind the bar were shelves that were designed to look like tree branches, holding the bottles. There were a few stools around the bar, a couple of which were already occupied, but the rest of the floor contained long tables and benches, where people could sit and mingle. The atmosphere of the bar was casual and respectful, and it was meant to be a place where people could hang out and have a good time. Wendy had never seen anyone step out of line, but she'd heard that Calie kept a baseball bat behind the bar just in case.

Standing behind the bar was Calie, who greeted them upon their arrival. As usual, she was wearing jeans and a striped shirt, with a backwards baseball cap perched on her short blond bob.

"How'd the show go tonight?" she asked as she poured their drinks.

"It was fabulous," Carina gushed.

"Went about as good as expected," Stacey said, waving a hand noncommittally.

"The audience enjoyed it," Wendy added helpfully.

"You'll have to check it out sometime," Stacey said.

Calie laughed. "If I ever decide to hire some help here, I'll do that."

Once they had their drinks—white wine for Wendy, red wine for Carina, and a Jack and cola for Stacey—they headed up to the third floor. This room had a more casual atmosphere, with chairs and small tables that could be arranged in whatever way was preferred, and the wooden floor was filled with scrapes from furniture being pulled here and there. There wasn't much about the room that resembled a treehouse, other than the wood panelling on the walls and a few lanterns hanging from the ceiling, but the windows offered a fantastic view down on Jacobi Street.

Music played lightly in the background, loud enough to provide atmosphere but low enough for people to carry on conversations without shouting. Samuel, Gerard, and Rhonda were already seated in a semi-circle, discussing their previous experiences in theatre, and the young women grabbed chairs and joined the group. The conversation opened to include them, but it soon became apparent that not everyone was interested in the dialogue anymore. After exchanging a few not-so-sly glances, Gerard and Carina made flimsy excuses to break away from the group and move to one of the more intimate corners of the room. The others exchanged knowing looks but continued with their conversation.

A short while later, Francesca showed up, and she instantly turned the focus her way. Carina and Gerard stayed in their corner, with Carina nervously glancing at Francesca every few seconds, but the blonde woman ignored her and joined the larger group, changing the topic of conversation to the show they'd just completed. Wendy noticed that Francesca was always her best self at the cast party, when she was celebrating with the others. Her energy was high, her mood positive, and it was one of the few times other troupe members found her approachable. Did it have something to do with the fact that Jim never went to these parties? Possibly, but Wendy couldn't be sure.

The group drank and laughed about the things that had gone wrong and mistakes that had been made, gently poking fun at each other. At first, Wendy used to be mortified every time she made a mistake, but then she realized that as long as the mistake didn't result in injury or damages, it was okay. In fact, some actors saw them as a challenge—a way to stretch their acting muscles. If something went wrong on stage and they were able to cover it up in such a way that the audience thought it was part of the show, then that would be worth a large pat on the back.

Eventually Betty, Galia, Billy, Paloma, and Ari arrived. The top floor became more crowded, the voices more animated, and the party swung into full gear. The alcohol was flowing and inside jokes were tossed around with no explanation. Occasionally they'd play a theatre game, or someone would try to teach someone else a dance from a show they'd once been in, but everything was always in good fun. The troupe worked hard to get the variety shows up and running, so they partied even harder.

While Francesca regaled the group about the time she'd accidentally walked on for the wrong scene during *The Importance of Being Ernest* and had to pretend that it was deliberate until she could find a good time to scurry offstage, Wendy chanced a look over at Betty. She was standing next to Galia, holding a glass of wine. When Betty caught her gaze, Wendy smiled and raised her glass in a cheers, and although Betty smiled and gave a cheers back, she remained at Galia's side for the rest of the night.

The party went on for a few more hours before people started breaking off to go home. Some of the actors would remain until Calie kicked them out in the wee hours of the morning, but others were concerned about the auditions tomorrow afternoon. Despite being able to cast a show in two seconds due to the small troupe size, Jim took auditions very seriously and expected everyone to show up and do their best. Tales were told of the time Gerard arrived at his audition and said, "I'm going to get the part anyway, so I won't bother wasting your time," then walked offstage. Jim had been so angry that he rewrote the entire play, taking out the character Gerard would have played and casting him in a non-speaking background role.

Wendy wasn't feeling particularly tired when she excused herself from the party, but she wanted to spend an hour or so practising her monologue before going to bed. She'd done as Francesca had suggested and created a monologue from *Dracula* by cutting out the other character's lines in between Mina's. It was short, about one minute long, but it showed Mina's vulnerability, fear, and strength—qualities which were reminiscent of a certain character in *Phantom*.

Although she still refused to say it out loud, she really wanted the part of Christine—wanted it so badly that she could feel it ache deep inside. As new as she was to acting, she desperately craved a chance to be in the spotlight and prove that she was more than a secondary character.

CHAPTER EIGHT

Before heading home, Paloma went back to the theatre to empty the dryer. There was always a large pile of costumes that needed to be washed after one of these shows, and there was only one washer and dryer in the entire building. Most of it could wait until tomorrow, but some pieces needed to be washed immediately so that they didn't sour, and then hung up after drying so that they wouldn't wrinkle. Luckily these were the kinds of tasks that she didn't need to be sober to perform.

Paloma was the only person in the theatre's costume department and had been for the past ten years. All the design teams were comprised of one person, and although the variety shows were insane and complicated, it wasn't anything that they weren't able to handle on their own. The theatre had a good-sized wardrobe collection that was comprised of outfits Paloma had discovered at second hand stores and costume sales from larger theatres, as well as pieces she'd created herself. She enjoyed being the master of costumes and having it all to herself.

After Jim announced that he was planning on doing *Phantom*, her mind went wild with all the possibilities.

She'd attended the musical when she was younger, and the costumes were so rich and extravagant. It was the complete opposite of *Glengarry Glen Ross*, where she'd merely needed suits and a police officer outfit. Although Paloma didn't yet know the particulars of the script that Jim was writing, he'd have to be a fool to remove the masquerade scene. Just like the dramatic chandelier fall, you couldn't have a *Phantom* story without it—it would be almost as bad as leaving out the Phantom himself.

Using her key to enter the theatre, she locked the door behind her, just as she'd promised Ari. All the design team had keys to the theatre, but they'd only received them after swearing to their stage manager that they wouldn't mess with anything, and that they'd be thorough when locking up. At times Paloma thought that Ari was being unreasonable with how much control they had over the theatre, but then she'd think about what it would be like if everyone came and went whenever they wanted and had to concede that this way was better.

The lobby was dark, except for a few soft night-lights that were plugged into the walls. As fun as it was to have a hive of activity around her, Paloma enjoyed those peaceful times at the theatre, when it was quiet and unassuming. It was like the entire building was hers and hers alone (although in the back of her mind she knew that Jim was upstairs drowning his sorrows in alcohol). Sometimes there were so many people bustling around that it was difficult to think, but in the darkness and solitude it was all hers.

Making her way into the auditorium, she saw the ghost light shining on the stage. The stage was empty except for the light, which stood at the centre—a single light bulb on a four-foot stand. Paloma didn't understand why they needed to put out a ghost light every night but had to admit that there was a kind of beauty about it.

Once she made her way to the lower level, she began turning on lights to see. Although she knew this floor well, she also knew that people were likely to leave things lying around in strange places, and it was better to see where you were going than to risk tripping over something and turning an ankle—especially when one's reflexes had been properly dulled.

After taking the clothes out of the dryer and hanging them up, Paloma looked at the racks of clothing lining the costume room. She'd have to do up some sketches and start thinking about fabrics. The dresses that she'd need for *Phantom* would have to be made from scratch or pieced together from older costumes. She'd also have to find a way to source formal tuxedos that didn't cost an arm and a leg but also looked expensive. For this show, she was definitely thinking tails.

A loud knocking noise startled her and she jumped. Taking in a deep breath, she told herself that it was only the furnace. Whatever they'd done to stop it from making the noise earlier must have worn off. She'd have to remember to tell Jim about it the next time she saw him.

Although the night was already growing late, Paloma pulled out one of her many bins of fabric and started looking through the contents, hoping to find some inspiration. She was holding up a bolt of pink satin fabric when there was another loud knock. She jumped again, and then laughed at herself for being so easily startled. However, when a third knock came soon after, she began to feel uneasy. The noises before had always been spaced out, with enough time in between to forget you'd heard it in the first place. Another knock sounded, and she began to wonder if there was something terribly wrong with the furnace. Was she in danger of it exploding? Perhaps it'd be best to go home.

She put the fabric down and stepped out of the costume room, turning off the lights after her. As she approached the staircase, she noticed that the door to the basement was ajar and that there was a red light coming from inside. She couldn't remember if the door had been open when she first passed it, but it must have been. She must not have noticed.

Suddenly a loud scraping sound startled her. She paused and listened. It sounded like someone was definitely down in the basement. Walking to the door, she opened it a little wider and listened again. It was hard to make out, but there were clanging sounds, like tools hitting metal, and something that almost sounded like a man muttering to himself. A feeling of ease washed over her. It was probably Billy. He was the resident handyman after all.

He must have come in after her, and she'd been too preoccupied with the costumes to hear him. That was what those noises were—Billy trying to fix the furnace. It didn't sound like he was being particularly successful, but what did she know about that kind of thing? Taking in a breath, Paloma turned to the staircase to leave.

Suddenly she heard a crash, like something heavy breaking off and falling to the floor. Instinct kicked in, sobering her up almost instantly, and she hurried to the basement. When she turned on the lights, only a few of the bulbs lit up. Some of them flickered in a way that indicated they would soon burn out, but it didn't slow her descent. Thankfully, the red glow from the furnace provided enough light for her to make out most of the room.

Stepping onto the floor, she called out Billy's name, letting him know that she was here and to tell her where he was. He didn't answer, but she could hear groans coming from the back of the room, where the furnace was. As she neared, she could feel the temperature of the room rising. She called out Billy's name, but still couldn't see him, and it was getting harder to hear him as the furnace's hissing and churning grew louder and louder.

"Billy? Where are you?" Once she reached the furnace, she saw nothing that looked like it could have caused that noise. Nothing seemed to have tipped over or fallen. Had she imagined it?

Suddenly there was a knock, the loudest one she'd heard yet, as if someone had slammed a baseball bat into the side of the furnace. Before the sound had a chance to finish reverberating, there was another and then another. The knocking was almost deafening, and even though Paloma tried to cover her ears with her hands, the noise wouldn't lessen. It felt like the room was going to fall in on itself, crumbling with her inside of it.

She tried to turn around and leave, but her feet wouldn't obey. Suddenly, the lights overhead started to flicker, and Paloma felt a shiver of fear run through her body. Her heart beat faster, and though she desperately wanted to run away, her body still wouldn't obey her mind. She needed to get out of here. She needed to get out of here now.

A deep, ragged breathing sounded behind her, and although the last thing she wanted to do was look at whatever could make a noise like that, her body moved of its own accord. In the dim red light, she could just make out a large shape that rose from the shadows. The being was much too tall for an ordinary person—too broad and big and hulking. Her heart leapt in her throat as the creature began to move towards her, and a terrified scream escaped her lips.

CHAPTER NINE

When Wendy woke up the next morning, she knew that she'd had some kind of strange dream during the night, but the details started slipping away the moment she opened her eyes. Images that were once so clear started getting fuzzy and dissolving into nothingness, leaving her with only vague recollections, but she could definitely remember standing on a stage in a long white dress that looked similar to a nightgown and hearing music.

Was this a sign that she was going to get the part of Christine? The stage was empty and so was the audience—no, actually, there were some people sitting in the seats, but she couldn't make out any faces. She knew that they were staring at her, but there was something strange about them. Were they wearing costumes? Maybe it was Stacey and Carina watching her, jealous because she'd gotten the part that they'd wanted.

Deciding to leave it alone, she told herself that it was likely a sign she was spending too much time thinking about the show. Her time would be better spent warming up her voice, instead of trying to interpret a half-remembered dream.

After eating a light breakfast—which was more like brunch, considering that it was closer to noon—she did a few vocal exercises and stretches before going over her monologue and song. Once she felt comfortable about both of them, she went to her closet and stood in front of it, trying to figure out what to wear. She didn't want to give the impression that she was wearing a costume, but wanted Jim to think of her as a young ingenue, so settled on a light blue dress with cap sleeves. After that decision had been made, she went over her monologue and song again before doing some breathing exercises as she anxiously waited for her audition time to get here.

When it was time to leave her apartment, she felt a thrill of excitement and a sense of trepidation. She usually felt nervous walking to an audition, but this time was different. It felt like there was more at stake. Normally she wouldn't care what part she received, but Francesca's encouragement had made her believe that she could get the lead. If she didn't, she'd be letting down not only herself but also Francesca and all of her teachings.

She arrived at the theatre early and quietly sneaked into the auditorium to sit in the back row. Samuel had just started his monologue, with Jim watching from the third row. Rumour had it that Samuel only had two monologues—one for comedy and one for drama—and this was the dramatic monologue. As he performed, Wendy figured that Samuel would be good as one of the managers of the theatre but definitely wasn't right for the Phantom. His posture was too stiff, and he wasn't menacing enough. Gerard would be a better Phantom, plus it'd keep him from being cast as Raoul. She smiled as a thought struck her. Maybe Raoul could be written out and the love story could be between Christine and Meg Giry. Then Betty could audition for Meg and the two of them could be together in front of everyone...

She heard her name being called and realized that she'd missed the end of Samuel's audition. Taking in a deep breath, Wendy stood up and made her way to the stage, preparing herself for what was to come.

And then, in a matter of minutes, it was over.

As she walked off the stage, she couldn't help noticing how many hours she'd spent agonizing over something that only lasted a few minutes. First Jim asked her for her monologue and, when that was finished, he asked her to sing. Then he thanked her for coming, and suddenly it was all over.

Wendy felt like she'd done a good job. There were no stumbles or forgotten lines, and the emotion she'd brought out had felt real enough. Jim hadn't shown much, but he did raise an eyebrow in surprise when she started singing. If she didn't get the part of Christine, at least she knew that she'd done her best.

On her way out of the auditorium, she was so relieved to be finished with her audition that she ran right into someone in the lobby. Backing up, she looked at a young man with dark, shaggy hair and darker eyes. He was wearing ripped jeans, a white t-shirt, and a black motorcycle jacket, like he'd just walked out of a James Dean movie.

"Sorry," she said, stepping out of his way. "Wasn't paying attention."

"Don't worry," he replied, shrugging one of his shoulders. "I'm a little lost. This is The Quaint Little Theatre, right?" He gestured at the lobby.

She nodded. "Yeah, it is."

"Great. Thanks." He moved past her and disappeared into the auditorium.

Wendy frowned at the space where he'd been standing. It was strange to see someone who wasn't part of the troupe in the theatre on a non-performance night. She thought back to the audition sheet, but there hadn't been any unfamiliar names on it—someone would have commented if there were. So, what was this guy doing here? Was he a walk-in? Then she remembered the strange knocking from a few days ago. Maybe he was here to check out the furnace and make sure everything was okay.

An involuntary shiver ran through her at the thought of the knocking, and she quickly made her way out of the theatre and into the bright afternoon sun.

CHAPTER TEN

As usual, Jim kept the casting secret until the very last minute. By early Friday evening everyone had received a message telling them that the read-through was at 1:00 pm on Saturday, and nothing else. Jim had once explained that giving actors the script or their parts beforehand gave them ill-conceived notions, but never actually explained what that meant or provided examples. Nobody felt strong enough about it to battle him on this matter, so they all let it go. It was simply one more quirk for an already quirk-laden director.

Wendy felt almost electric as she made her way to the theatre for the read-through. This was the moment she was both anticipating and dreading. The world wouldn't end if she didn't get the part she wanted, but she'd feel like a deflated balloon. It would be almost unbearable having to watch Stacey or Carina perform the part she so desperately wanted.

She arrived at the theatre five minutes before 1:00 pm. The stage had been cleared away of all set pieces and had a large square table in the centre, surrounded by chairs. In front of each chair was a pile of paper—the much-anticipated script. Despite the constant curiosity around it, nobody was sitting down or flipping through the pages. Instead, they huddled in groups, circling the table like sharks, wary of seeming too eager or getting too close.

Standing near the edge of the stage were Stacey and Carina. Wendy went over and, after a quick greeting, asked how their auditions had gone. It was partly because the conversation was expected, but also because she was hoping to gauge how well they'd done in relation to her. Carina had been surprised by the request for a song, but otherwise thought her audition had gone well, and Stacey felt that hers had been great. They asked Wendy about hers, and she said it had gone well, and then talked about how she'd caught part of Sam's audition, quickly changing the subject.

"Who is *that*?" Stacey interrupted, staring between Wendy and Carina. The two of them immediately turned around and Wendy saw the same young man she'd run into after her audition. He was wearing a similar outfit as yesterday, which was almost identical except for the jeans being slightly more faded. A cautious expression crossed his face as he looked around the theatre, taking it all in.

"*Me gusta...*" Carina said with a hungry smile on her face.

Wendy frowned in confusion. "What's the furnace guy doing here?"

"Wait, do you know him?" Stacey demanded, swiftly turning to her.

After shaking her head, Wendy shrugged. "I ran into him after my audition. Like, *literally* ran into him. I thought he was here to look at the furnace, but maybe not." Yesterday he'd walked around like he owned the place, but now he was more trepidatious.

"I hope he's playing Raoul," Carina said, watching as he made his way to the stage. "I don't even care if he can act."

The stranger walked over to Jim and they talked quietly as everyone else pretended not to stare. Wendy was certain that every conversation was now focused on this new addition.

The mood was broken as the auditorium doors swung open, and everyone turned to watch Francesca make her way towards the stage. Wendy had to give it to her—Francesca knew how to make an entrance.

"Seats, everyone," Ari called out.

Jim took his place at the "head" of the table, between Ari and Billy. He motioned for the new guy to take the seat closest to Ari, while everyone else made their way to their usual seats. Wendy normally sat next to Ari, so she was a bit put off by the new guy taking her seat, but then she noticed that this side of the table had four chairs instead of three. She'd been so entranced by the script that she hadn't even picked up on the change.

As she sat down between the new guy and Stacey, the young man turned to her and gave her a slight nod before looking down at the script in front of him.

Francesca arrived on the stage, taking the seat across from Wendy. She always showed up exactly five minutes late to every read-through, so it never started until she arrived. When Wendy asked her about this, Francesca said that the first five minutes was always filled with inane chatter and gossip, so she preferred to skip it.

Clearing his throat, Jim stood up and looked around the table. "I know that you have all been waiting impatiently for the cast list, but it happens that we have a new cast member joining us for this show." He gestured towards the young man, although it wasn't necessary. "So today will be a little different. I shall be introducing you at the same time as your character, and I will also be introducing the crew."

Jim stepped back from the table, and everyone kept their eyes on him as he moved around the stage, introducing each person.

"This is Ari, they are our stage manager. Billy, he is our set and lighting designer. Francesca, she will be playing Carlotta, Sorelli, and the nurse. Gerard, he will be our Phantom, as well as Monsieur Poligny. Samuel, he will be Monsieur Moncharmin. Scott, he is basically a gofer."

Wendy noticed that Scott's eyebrows furrowed at the job description and his head bowed even lower than it already was, attempting to hide his frown.

"Rhonda, she will be our accompanist and musical director. Paloma, she is our costume designer. Galia, she is in charge of special effects. Betty, she is in charge of props. Carina, she will be Mrs. Giry, Meg Giry, and Man One. Stacey, she is playing Remy, Jammes, and Man Two. Wendy, she will be Christine."

Wendy's eyes widened as she realized that she'd actually gotten the part of Christine. Although Carina and Stacey were playing other characters, Wendy hadn't realized what that meant for her until Jim had actually said it. A large grin broke out on her face, which she was quick to dial back to a modest smile, lest the others think she was gloating. When she glanced over at Francesca, the blonde woman gave her a proud look, and she had to fight to keep a blush from creeping up into her cheeks.

"And Vance, he will be our Raoul. I am Jim, he/him, and I am your director. And now that the introductions are out of the way, it is time for us to get to the script."

At the end of the read-through, Wendy couldn't wait to start rehearsals. Jim had created a script with all the expected romance, horror, and tension. He'd cut out a lot of characters from the novel and simplified the story and language, making it a tight, energetic show. There were some hints to the musical in it, but, according to Jim, it was still very much like the book.

Jim talked for a while about his vision for this show and what he expected of everyone. He mentioned that a few of the designers would be expected to dress up and stand around for the retirement and masquerade scenes to make the stage look more crowded. He also explained that since the opera in the show is *Faust*, Rhonda would be working on adapting the music into something more accessible for both the actors and the audience. The rest of the musical numbers would be songs from the musical version of *Phantom*, so that they would be familiar to both the singers and the audience. He intended to have all of the cast singing "Masquerade" for the masquerade scene but was prepared to use a recording of the song, should it not sound the way he wanted it to.

"Good to know we've got the rights," Rhonda said, a half-smile on her face that was more akin to a half-smirk.

Jim gave her a tired look but didn't respond. A few people around the table were holding back laughter, trying to hide their amusement. For theatres to perform certain shows or musicals they had to pay for the rights to do so, ensuring that those who created the works received compensation, but Jim never did. At first, he'd tried to do original works or plays that had no rights, but when he realized that nobody really knew or cared about the theatre, his morality went right out the window. Rights were expensive and the theatre wasn't exactly resting on a bed of money, so he figured that he was owed a certain level of oversight. Rhonda first enquired about it during a pared-down version of *My Fair Lady*, and Jim had told her that if the rights holders wanted him to pay, then they could march right down to the theatre and demand the money in person. He knew that this theatre was small enough to go unnoticed—both a blessing and a curse. And, sure enough, he'd gotten away with it so far. While Wendy didn't know much about producing theatre, she also wasn't the person making the decisions, so if anyone got in trouble, it wouldn't be her. If anything, she was glad that the music for this show would mostly be songs she already knew how to sing.

Jim finished his ramble and declared the read-through over. Before everyone could leave, Ari handed out a rehearsal schedule, reminding them all to pay close attention. Jim warned them that tomorrow would be their only day off next week, so they should spend the time going over the script to be prepared for when rehearsals started. They only had two and a half weeks to rehearse, so the sooner they were off-book, the better. Then he asked

Vance if the two of them could have a word, to which Vance nodded.

"Let's go," Stacey said to Carina and Wendy, and the two nodded, grabbing their scripts as they stood up from the table. Wendy glanced towards Betty, but she was deep in conversation with her sister, probably about the many effects and props that the show would require.

The group left the theatre and headed to The Belle Verde for their traditional after-read-through meal. They were early for supper, which was good because they'd stand a chance of getting a booth and not have to sit at the bar, which was smack in the centre of the restaurant, or one of the tables around the room, which were always too cramped. Gossiping was best done in a booth, where you didn't have patrons and staff constantly manoeuvring around you and possibly listening in.

Gradey, one of the waiters who always seemed to be at the restaurant no matter what time of day it was, greeted them with a Southern-twang-tinged "How y'all doing?" As had become their custom, Stacey replied in English, Wendy in French, and Carina in Spanish. Gradey gave them a half-grin and showed them to a booth along the right side, giving them menus despite the fact that nobody who lived on Jacobi Street ever looked at them. The menu was basically the size of a phonebook and it was almost guaranteed that whatever meal you wanted was inside, no matter how obscure it might be. And if it weren't there, there was a good chance that you could cobble together a few different dishes to make it.

"What can I get you?" he asked, his voice now a more neutral accent than the greeting had been. Not that he needed to ask, since everyone basically ordered the same thing every time, but he always did anyway.

"*Ropa Vieja*," Carina said.

"Pastrami on rye," Stacey ordered. "With lightly salted potato chips and carrot sticks on the side."

Wendy paused. "I'll get the cranberry spinach salad with chicken."

Gradey raised an eyebrow. "Sounds like *someone* got a good part in the next play." He smiled at her and walked away, not bothering to wait for a reply.

"Nerves getting to you?" Stacey asked. "It's your first big role, after all."

Wendy nodded. "A bit." Normally she'd order *navarin d'agneau* with a side of bannock, but after all the excitement today her stomach needed something lighter. It had become a tradition for Stacey and Carina to go to The Belle Verde after every read-through, and after Wendy joined the troupe, they'd invited her to come along. Most of the time they'd get their usual dish, but once in a while Stacey or Carina would order a salad after getting cast in a really good role, being too nervous and excited for their usual order. The first time it happened it had thrown Gradey for a loop, but he quickly caught on. Wendy realized that this was the first time she'd been able to do this, and that satisfaction helped calm her nerves a little.

"You'll be fine," Stacey said. "Jim wouldn't give you the part if he didn't think you could handle it. I mean, it'd only be more work for him."

"Um, thanks?"

Stacey waved her hand, dismissing her words. "Just chalk what I say down to being a jealous bitch because I wanted to play Christine. Especially since you get the new hot guy to be your Raoul."

Carina sighed wistfully. "He's got a real James Dean vibe going on. It's so hot."

"It's a good thing I have a weak spot for broody guys," Stacey added.

Although those two seemed enamoured of the new arrival, Wendy wasn't sure what to make of Vance. He'd barely said anything that wasn't written in his script during the read-through and didn't try to get to know anyone. At least he sounded good reading the lines, which hopefully meant that he could act.

While the others gushed about how hot Vance was, Wendy found it difficult to join in. Perhaps she'd have found it easier if she only had to admire him from afar, but he was her main scene partner. If he turned out to be a major jerk or a terrible actor, her dream role would quickly turn into a nightmare.

Gradey arrived with their drinks, placing each one down with emphasis before moving on to another table. Unlike food, they never bothered ordering drinks. Beer was the assumed libation of The Belle Verde, and Gradey always knew what to give them. Wendy had a light, white beer with citrus notes, Carina had a Mexican beer that came in a tall green bottle, and Stacey had a beer so dark that light couldn't penetrate it.

"You know, Paloma seemed tired today," Carina said, sipping her drink in a way that seemed to suggest she'd take in fewer calories if she took smaller sips. "There were bags under her eyes, and she looked pale. Do you think she's coming down with something?"

"I hope not," Wendy frowned. If one person in the theatre got sick then it was bound to spread to everyone else, and she didn't want to come down with a cold or flu this early into rehearsals. She made a mental note to stock up on vitamin C. "Hopefully it's just a hangover or a bad night's rest."

Stacey nodded in agreement. "Oh, did either of you notice that Scott seemed extra squirrelly today? That guy is so weird."

"It probably had something to do with Jim calling him a gofer," Wendy said, laughing at the memory.

Carina joined in. "I swear, the day that Jim describes him as his assistant director is the day that I keel over dead from shock."

"If that ever happens, I'm sure Jim will be the next one to keel over," Stacey added as they all laughed.

"I wonder what the chandelier drop is going to look like," Wendy said, trying to picture something so crazy happening in their small theatre.

Carina nearly snorted. "We'll be lucky if it doesn't drop on our heads."

"You know Ari wouldn't let anything like that happen," she replied pointedly.

"I also know that Galia is insane," Carina deftly countered. "Remember the time she caught the stage on fire during that wrestling skit?"

Wendy winced at the memory; the past five months having done nothing to dull it. The skit had been about a fearsome wrestler whose only fear was fire, and it was supposed to have four pyrotechnic charges go off while he was gloating about his big win, reducing him to a quivering, weeping mess. But instead of the small charges that Ari had approved, on the night of the show Galia decided to make them extra theatrical. It resulted in actual surprise from Gerard, who was playing the wrestler, and then real fear as the ropes making up the wrestling ring around him caught on fire. Ari had to bring in the fire curtain while Billy ran for a fire extinguisher. Luckily, the audience thought it was all part of the show and Gerard escaped with no injuries.

That stunt had almost resulted in Galia getting fired, but instead she'd been given a severe talking to and a second chance. With the watchful eye of Ari hanging over her, Galia had been much less reckless ever since.

Stacey took a long drink from her glass before bringing it down onto the table with a thump. "I wanna talk about the theatre ghost!"

Wendy and Carina exchanged a confused look.

"What ghost?" Carina asked.

"The ghost of The Quaint Little Theatre!" Stacey looked at them expectantly but received blank looks. "Look, I've been doing some digging and although I haven't found anything about a specific ghost that haunts the theatre, I've found allusions to a few people who've died there over the years. A stagehand here, an actor there, an audience member once in a while. There are a lot of ghosts that could be haunting the building."

Carina gave her a sceptical look.

Wendy frowned. "But Francesca said that there hasn't been a ghost at the theatre since Jim bought it fifteen years ago. You'd think someone would notice if there was."

"Ah ha!" Stacey exclaimed, pointing a finger at Wendy for emphasis. "I have a theory about that! See, I think that the ghosts within the theatre have been lying dormant, probably because they don't have enough energy to manifest. But when Jim decided to do *Phantom*, it woke them up. Like some kind of invocation. That's why we're hearing that knocking—it's the spirits trying to communicate with us!"

Carina burst out laughing. "You are *realmente loca*."

"The knocking was just the furnace, and it hasn't been heard since Wednesday," Wendy added. She was trying to sound flippant, but deep down she knew that there was something about the noise that unsettled her. Could it actually be ghosts trying to communicate with them by tapping on pipes? Didn't ghosts throw stuff or move things around? What kind of ghost knocked?

"Look, I can tell you're both sceptical," Stacey said, refusing to back down, "but I know that's what happened. Jim called up some kind of spirit and now it's trying to talk to us. We need to have a séance or something to communicate with it and find out what it wants, and then once we've helped it, it'll be able to rest."

Wendy exchanged another look with Carina. Both were equally doubtful about Stacey's theory, but before they could say anything, Gradey arrived with their meals. They all tucked in and Wendy hoped that it would put an end to the ghost talk, but Stacey seemed to take their silence as acceptance and continued to ramble while they ate, hypothesizing which ghost would be the likeliest to come forth. There had been a stagehand who'd fallen from the lighting grid and died, an audience member who'd had a heart attack during a show, an actor who'd killed themselves in their dressing room, an actor who'd killed another in a fit of jealousy, and a director who'd hung himself on stage.

Wendy tried to ignore Stacey while she ate, but it wasn't easy. She was glad that she'd ordered a salad, since the more Stacey talked the less she felt like eating. Thankfully, Stacey didn't go into any of the gory details, but she did speculate a lot about each ghost, making up stories about how they'd all met their demise. At one point, Wendy wondered if Stacey was suddenly so into this ghost theory because she didn't want to talk about how Wendy had taken the part they'd all wanted.

By the time they'd finished eating, the restaurant was starting to fill up with other inhabitants of Jacobi Street, so they quickly paid and left.

"See you later," Wendy said as they broke apart and went their separate ways. Carina and Stacey shared an apartment above The Soper Boutique, which was in the opposite direction as Wendy's apartment. They waved back to her before turning away, heads bent towards each other as they talked in low voices—mostly likely gossiping about Jim's casting choices.

Wendy couldn't help feeling relieved now that the other women were gone. Although she liked them, they hadn't given her much of a chance to feel excited about getting the lead role in the play. Stacey had hit the nail on the head about them being "jealous bitches," but it still would have been nice if they'd let her gush for a bit.

Taking in a deep breath, Wendy cleared away all thoughts of ghosts and jealous co-workers and allowed herself to think of how she'd finally managed to get a role that she'd desperately wanted—that everyone else had desperately wanted. A wide smile broke out on her face, and, as she walked towards her apartment, she felt a bounce in her step.

CHAPTER ELEVEN

Billy whistled to himself as he looked through the old set pieces stacked in the basement. Even though it was their day off, he'd come into the theatre to show Jim his preliminary sketches for the sets for *Phantom*, in order to get started on them right away. After Jim approved them (with only a few minor changes suggested), Billy had decided to go to the basement in the hopes that there would be some old pieces in storage that he'd be able to re-use. The show had nine different sets and Jim wanted them all to look luxurious and professional, so if Billy didn't have to make everything from scratch, it'd save him a lot of time.

Ever since their former scenic painter, Eddie, had decided to walk out on the job, Billy found himself having to fill in the role. He'd called Eddie's apartment to find out why, but his partner said that Eddie had gone and wasn't coming back. Billy wasn't sure why he would quit, especially right in the middle of a project, leaving behind a half-painted set piece and open cans of paint around the stage, but it was probably something serious like a family emergency. Jim hadn't found a satisfactory replacement yet and, knowing him, he was using this as an excuse not to spend money hiring someone. Although Billy wasn't as good a painter as Eddie, he was good enough for Jim not to complain.

As Billy searched through the large boards, he could hear a low knocking sound coming from the furnace. Shaking his head, he wondered when Jim would get someone in to look at it. It probably wasn't anything serious, but it wouldn't hurt to fix whatever was making the sound and reassure everyone that the place wasn't about to blow up. It was likely a cost issue, as Jim hated spending money on anything that wasn't show-related, but keeping the building in tip-top shape was important. It'd be hard to stage a play in a building that was falling apart.

He pulled out a large board that had been painted to look like a stone wall and set it aside with the other pieces he'd pulled. So far, he had pieces that could be used for the manager's office, cemetery, and now the catacombs. It wasn't much, but it was a start. And the less time he spent painting sets, the more he'd have to work on Box 5, the eponymous box that the Phantom requested be held for him for every performance.

Suddenly Billy stopped whistling. He thought he'd heard something, but when he paused to listen all he could hear was the sound of the furnace. Shrugging, he went back to his work, looking through the flats. When he was finished with that, he moved over to the set pieces on the other side of the room. He needed to find something that could be used for the mirrored cabinet in Christine's dressing room. It had to be big enough for people to travel through, and sturdy enough to stand up to a lot of activity, as well as whatever Galia had in mind for that effect.

Pausing again, he stepped out into the middle of the room and looked towards the back, where the furnace was. He'd definitely heard something that time, but who could be back there? Nobody else had been around when he'd arrived at the theatre.

Maybe Jim had come down earlier to look at the furnace and had injured himself. It wasn't likely, but who else could it be?

"Jim? Is that you?" Billy called out.

There was no answer, other than a sharp knock. He nervously ran a hand through his thick brown hair, before tugging at his bushy beard. The knock sounded again.

"Is anyone back there?" he called out.

Another knock.

He was about to turn back to his work when he heard a pained moaning.

"Don't worry, I'm on my way!" he said as he hurried to the back of the room. When he approached the large metal furnace, he scanned the area for the injured person, but there were only shadows amongst the glowing red light. Looking up, he noticed that some of the fluorescent lights in the ceiling were dark, and he made a quick mental note to replace them later.

"Where are you?" he called out. "Am I close?"

There was no answer except for a loud knock, and Billy was hit with a sudden realization that the knocking might have been someone crying out for help. All this time they had no idea that a person was down here, hoping that someone would come and help them.

Another knock followed that one, and Billy stepped

closer to the furnace, moving in the direction of the sound, keeping his eyes out for an arm or leg trapped underneath something. The knocking grew louder and more frequent, which he took as a sign that he was on the right path.

"Don't worry," he called out, trying to be heard over the knocking. "I'm here to help!"

The air began to grow hotter as he manoeuvred around the large metal furnace, moving towards the back wall. Wiping the sweat from his brow, Billy searched desperately, but it was almost impossible to make out anything in the dim red light.

The knocking increased in intensity and suddenly seemed to be coming from everywhere at once. The heat was getting worse, but he had to find the person in trouble and help them.

"Where are you?" he asked, resisting the urge to put his hands over his ears and drown out the noise.

Looking around frantically, he suddenly noticed movement in the far corner.

"Just hold on!" he called out as he headed towards the corner, walking deeper into the thick, dark shadows, which quickly rose to swallow him.

CHAPTER TWELVE

Wendy woke up twenty minutes before her alarm went off and nearly jumped out of bed with excitement. Unlike when she'd first started at the theatre, today she felt both prepared and qualified for the job she was about to do.

There was a vague notion in the back of her mind that she'd had the same odd dream of her standing on stage and being watched by an invisible audience, but she tried not to give it any thought. Now that she'd gotten her desired role, the dream had probably transformed into the kind where she'd forgotten her lines in the middle of a performance or came to rehearsal only to discover that Jim had replaced her with someone else, and she didn't need any negative thoughts or insecurities influencing her mood today. Today was about being positive.

She'd read through the script multiple times on Sunday, even though it was her day off, because she wanted to prove to Jim that he hadn't made a mistake in giving her this role. Not only was she well on her way to memorizing all her lines, but she had a good glimpse into Christine's motives, actions, and emotions.

Some of her preparedness came at a small cost, though. Betty had come over last night to spend a few hours, and while the two were watching a movie, she caught Wendy constantly sneaking looks at her script instead. Thankfully, Betty understood the situation, and after some playful chastising, she turned her attention to the movie and said nothing more about Wendy's inability to keep her eyes off her lines.

As Wendy approached the theatre for her first day of *Phantom* rehearsal, she could feel her heart racing with anticipation. Stepping into the lobby, she noticed that Scott was sitting in a chair near the door to the auditorium, holding his ever-present clipboard with one hand and a pen in the other. He was attempting to sit up straight and proper, but his shoulders were slumped and there was a wash of irritation on his face—likely from having to be the designated door-watcher. She gave him a smile before walking past but didn't say anything because she didn't want to give him an invitation to complain.

Swiftly making her way through the auditorium and the backstage area, she only slowed down when she reached the staircase. Pausing for a moment, she was unable to stop herself from looking at the door which led down to the lower level, where the door to the basement was located. Stacey's words about the many ghosts that might be haunting the theatre and trying to communicate with them echoed in her mind, but she quickly pushed them aside and ascended the stairs.

The rehearsal hall was the only room above the backstage area. It was as wide as the stage (including the wings) and one-and-a-half times as long, so it didn't feel crowded unless all of the actors and set pieces were piled inside. The floor had already been marked with different colours of spike tape that outlined the stage area and showed where certain set pieces, like the infamous Box 5, would be located. The floor was relatively clean, but Wendy knew that more pieces of colourful tape would make their way onto the floor as they rehearsed, marking the location of furniture and other smaller pieces.

Ari and Jim were already in the room, with Ari sitting at a table near the back, in the "audience" section of the room. Their giant binder was open in front of them, containing the full script, paper for notes, and more paper—just in case. Next to it was a case holding pencils, pens, erasers, and more labels and tabs than Wendy would ever know what to do with. Ari was in discussion with Jim, who stood in front of the table, his back to the door. Wendy greeted them both, and although Ari said "hello," Jim merely looked at her and nodded before turning back to the conversation.

When Wendy first met Ari, she didn't know what to make of them. They were five foot eight and broad, with a muscular physique that made you suspect that you shouldn't underestimate them. Their hair was bright pink, straight and long, and the right side was shaved down to the skin. They usually wore their hair flipped to the left, exposing the shaved part, and revealing an ear that had piercings all the way from the bottom to the top. There was something so punk about the ear piercings, especially when paired with the silver hoop pierced through their lip. Ari usually wore tank tops, jeans, and steel-toed boots, no matter the season, which only added to their tough aesthetic. Wendy sometimes felt jealous of Ari's style, although she knew she'd never be able to pull something like that off.

Usually, Ari didn't say much during rehearsals, which made the occasions when they spoke all the more important. Oftentimes they'd mutter to themselves in German when annoyed or irritated, but they never let their emotions boil over—unlike certain other people in the troupe. Everyone respected Ari, and nobody crossed them. Despite all of this, Ari had a great sense of humour and was great to talk to outside of rehearsal. They had all kinds of stories about working in theatres in Berlin—from classical to modern to extremely experimental. The parties at the Treehouse didn't usually pick up until they arrived.

Wendy spotted two empty chairs facing the table, which were likely for her and Vance. More chairs were stacked along the side of the room, and although there weren't any set pieces up here yet, there was a stack of black wooden boxes in one corner that they could use in place of items. Rhonda wasn't needed at this rehearsal, so the piano was tucked away in the far corner. Taking a seat, Wendy opened her script and went over her lines as she waited for Vance to arrive.

He showed up a few minutes later, just before the call time. He gave a quick hello to everyone in the room before taking the seat next to Wendy.

"Well, let's get started," Jim said, sitting down next to Ari.

Ari tapped their pencil on a nearby piece of paper, drawing Jim's attention. He looked down at the paper, frowned slightly, and cleared his throat.

"Before we get down to business," Jim said, addressing Wendy and Vance, "you should take a moment to get to know each other. You two will be sharing a lot of scenes together, so I don't want either of you feeling uncomfortable. Take the next five—"

Ari coughed loudly.

"Take the next *ten* minutes to get comfortable with each other." Jim took in a breath and attempted a smile. "After all, trust behind the stage leads to greater trust on stage."

Wendy noticed that one corner of Ari's mouth had quirked up into a half-smile. No doubt they'd been the one to let Jim know that it wasn't wise to hire a stranger and drop them into the troupe without any introductions. She wouldn't have been surprised to find out that Jim was quoting Ari for that last bit.

As Jim and Ari started talking amongst themselves again, Wendy turned to Vance and gave what she hoped was a warm smile. He looked at her, his mouth moving up into a quick smile before going back to neutral.

"I'm Wendy," she said, holding out her hand. "I've been with the troupe for about half a year, and I live on Jacobi Street."

He looked at her hand for a few seconds before shaking it. "I'm Vance. I did some acting in high school, but this is my first professional role. I mean, if this counts as professional. I know it's not Broadway or anything, but..." he paused. "I live up on 28th."

"So, how did you get involved in all of this?" she asked.

"I saw a flier on 13th Street."

She waited for him to elaborate, but he didn't. "That's how I got here, too," she said. "I used to work at East of Sicily, but I saw a flier and decided to audition."

He nodded and Wendy had to resist sighing. This guy really wasn't giving her much to work with.

"I wasn't much of an actor when I started," she rambled, "but they hired me anyway. After a few shows I realized how fun this was and how much I enjoyed it, so I started taking lessons and stuff. So, why'd you decide to accept the part?"

"Well," he said, his voice uncertain, "I wanted to try something new. Work's been a bit... tedious. Like I said, I used to act in high school but had to give up after graduation. And I like the novel, so I figured this might be fun to try."

Wendy nodded and smiled, thankful to get more than a few words out of him. For a guy that wanted to do something fun, he was surprisingly lacklustre. But being stuck with a dull scene-partner was still better than getting stuck with Gerard or Sam, or—heaven forbid—Scott.

She asked a few more leading questions, and it felt like he was starting to warm up to her by the end of the ten minutes. She'd learned about some of the parts he'd had in other plays, and how the garage he worked at was owned by his father, and even that he was currently seeing someone. It was a lot of surface-level information, but at least she had a better idea of who he was. Although she doubted that they'd ever be best friends, she was fairly certain he wasn't an axe murderer.

"We'll read through the scene once," Jim instructed them. "When we are done, you may ask questions, and

I will give notes. Then we'll read it again. And then we'll get up on our feet." He looked at them for agreement, and they both nodded.

Wendy and Vance read through their first scene together, which was the first time Raoul and Christine meet. It was a great scene because Raoul was so excited to see his childhood friend, but Christine had to pretend not to recognize him because the Phantom was nearby, listening. The scene had more to it—with Raoul coming back to try and talk to Christine one more time, but instead he hears her speaking with the Phantom, and then he sees two men carrying a body along the hall—but those parts would be rehearsed later, when the other actors were around. Instead, they moved on to the next scene with the two of them, when Raoul finds Christine in a cemetery, going to lay flowers on her father's grave.

Their rehearsal had been scheduled for four hours, with a break in the middle, and by the end of it, they'd loosely blocked all of Christine and Raoul's scenes. Wendy was sure to take meticulous notes in pencil, knowing full well that Jim might end up changing everything during the next rehearsal. She'd been surprised by Vance, who seemed to become a whole other person during their scenes. His first read wasn't anything to call home about, but by the time they got on their feet he was much more comfortable and warmer. She could see why Jim hired him.

After their rehearsal time was over, Ari informed Wendy and Vance that Paloma would be expecting the two of them at wardrobe for their costume measuring. Wendy thanked Ari and headed out of the room.

"Um... Wendy?"

She paused at the top of the stairs, turning around at the sound of her name. Vance was standing behind her, looking sheepish.

"Can I ask you where the wardrobe room is?" he said.

"Just follow me," she replied.

Vance didn't say much as she led him down to the lower level and through the hall, so she tried to fill up the silence by talking about the theatre and pointing out where everything was. When they reached the costume room, she was thankful for the opportunity to stop talking.

Paloma informed them that she'd measure Vance first and asked Wendy to wait out in the hall, to give them some privacy. While she waited, Wendy tried to distract herself by thinking about where she'd get something to eat for lunch. It'd be in her best interest to learn how to cook better, but she was always missing some vital ingredient in her cupboards or she'd read a recipe wrong and it would always taste a little strange. It was much less hassle to let someone else do the cooking, especially when they were much better at it than her.

A loud knock startled her from her thoughts and her heart jumped. Memories of Stacey's ghost stories started to creep forward, filling her imagination with images of spirits desperately trying to communicate, but she shoved them back into the far recesses of her mind. It was only air in the pipes, nothing more.

Another knock sounded, and it was so loud that it seemed to reverberate throughout the building. Wendy looked around, but she was the only person standing in the hallway and nobody else poked their head out from any of the rooms. How had nobody else heard that? For a brief moment she considered asking Paloma and Vance if they'd heard the sound but decided that they might think she was being paranoid.

She tried to calm herself down and tell herself that there was nothing supernatural about the sounds, but the knocking continued the entire time she was waiting. Sometimes it was sharp and quick, and other times low and deep. It sounded like it was coming from different places, and sometimes all around her. Still, nobody else came out to enquire about it, making her wonder if only she could hear it.

Was it possible that Stacey's crazy stories were true? Was there some kind of strange presence in the theatre? If so, what was it trying to say? Did the different knocks mean different things?

But if it was simply a lonely ghost with unfinished business, why did every sound unnerve her? Why did it feel like there was some kind of malevolent spirit watching her with unseen eyes? Wendy wrapped her arms around herself and tried to tune out the noise.

When Paloma poked her head out to tell her it was her turn, she was so relieved that she could have kissed the woman. Vance thanked Wendy as he left, heading down the hallway, and she hoped that he'd be able to find his way out okay. She hurried into the costume room, finding Paloma leaning on one of the tables.

"How was rehearsal, my dear?" Paloma asked, grabbing her tape measure and pushing herself upright. There were dark circles under her eyes and her movements were slower than usual.

"It was good. How are you, Paloma?" she asked gently.

"Good," Paloma said, before realizing that Wendy hadn't asked just to be kind. "I've had some trouble sleeping, but it's nothing, *mi querido*. I have too many costumes to make to let something like that bother me."

Wendy smiled. "Well, I hope your sleep troubles end soon."

"They usually do."

The two chatted as Paloma measured her, comparing her current measurements with the ones from last month's show and overwriting anything that needed to be changed. Although Paloma was clearly exhausted by the time they finished, she decided to show Wendy some of the sketches she'd made for Christine's costumes, which seemed to breathe new life into her and renew her energy. Wendy gushed over the costumes, growing even more excited about the role, and she could see that Paloma was delighted by her reaction. When they were done, Wendy wished her a peaceful sleep tonight and headed out.

As she walked along the hallway, Wendy kept her ears open and her guard up. The knocking seemed to have stopped, but she quickened her pace anyway, hastily making her way upstairs.

CHAPTER THIRTEEN

"Betty! I need your help testing the noose!"

Betty jolted up from the book she was diligently working on, almost knocking it to the floor. Despite having spent the past hour carefully distressing the pages to make it look like it was from the early nineteen-hundreds, she immediately lost interest in her project and rushed into the hallway.

"No, no, no, no, no," she muttered under her breath as she hurried to the special effects room. When she entered the room, she saw her sister standing on a chair, a noose around her neck. "Galia!" she cried out a split second before her sister stepped off the chair.

The noose tightened around Galia's throat and she started to flail as her airway was constricted. Betty rushed forward and grabbed her sister around the legs, getting a few kicks to the midsection before containing them, and guided her back onto the chair.

"What were you thinking?" Betty scolded her sister once she was breathing again. "Jim said that it's supposed to be a dummy in the noose, not a real person!"

"I was testing the weight capabilities," Galia said, taking the noose off and rubbing her throat. She'd only been hanging for a few seconds, but her voice was strained. "If it can hold me without breaking, then it should be able to hold whatever dummy you come up with, provided that it's under my weight." She paused. "Although the dummy will be hanging for a while, so I should test it for longer."

"Dammit, sis," Betty cried out. "Test it with a dummy, not yourself! What if I hadn't been here? Or hadn't heard you?"

"I had a backup plan," Galia said flippantly, smoothing her chin-length blond hair with both hands. Her response didn't inspire much relief. Although Galia was older and taller and more confident, Betty often felt that she was missing the gene for self-preservation.

"Shouldn't you be working on the chandelier?" Betty asked. "That's going to be way harder to coordinate than a noose."

Galia looked up at the rope and grabbed it with one hand, giving it a tug. There was a bit of slack, but not much, and the rope stayed strong. She nodded satisfactorily, put her other hand on it, and lifted herself off the chair. After swinging for a minute, she smiled broadly before dropping to the floor.

"I mean, hanging by an arm isn't the same as hanging by a neck, but if it can support that kind of weight, we should be okay..." her voice trailed off as she did a few sums in her head.

"The chandelier, sis?" Betty prompted.

"Yeah, I'm working on it..."

"Good, because that drop at the end of Act 1 needs to be fantastic."

Galia's green eyes widened with excitement. "Oh, it's gonna be *so* cool."

Shaking her head, Betty watched her sister lose all interest in the noose and wander over to her drafting table. Now that her attention was somewhere else, Betty moved the ladder from the corner of the room and climbed up it to untie the noose. The knots were difficult to untie, due to the stress having tightened them, but eventually she managed to get the rope down from the beam without cutting it. The entire time she worked, Galia said nothing to her, her head filled with thoughts of chandeliers falling.

"I'm taking this with me so that I can test it on the dummy," Betty called out as she descended the ladder with the noose.

Her sister gave a half-hearted wave, not bothering to look up.

She sighed and put the ladder away before heading back to the props room. She wished that Jim hadn't decided on a play with so much going on. There were a lot of different and dangerous elements involved, and she was worried that her sister was going to destroy the theatre— or herself—trying to pull these effects off. She still remembered last Christmas when Galia was trying to figure out a pyrotechnic effect for their production of *A Christmas Carol* and accidentally set herself on fire—four times. In order to prevent her sister from ending up in the hospital or burning the theatre down, she'd had to get Ari to intervene.

Placing the noose somewhere her sister wouldn't find it, Betty went back to work on the journal. Once it was distressed enough, she'd be able to start writing in it. Jim had given her detailed notes on what the journal should look like and she knew that he expected her to follow them to the letter, even though ninety-nine percent of the audience wouldn't be able to see any of those fine details. She could have made a few pages look great and skimped on the rest, but she didn't want to risk Jim seeing those bad pages and thinking she was lazy.

After thirty minutes, she looked at her watch and saw that it was getting close to dinnertime. Wendy would be expecting her soon. Betty put away her work and started to leave, but she paused outside the special effects room. Peeking in, she could see that her sister was still hunched over the chandelier plans.

"Umm, I've got plans tonight, so I won't be home," she said through the doorway. Her right hand absentmindedly tugged at the hair around her ear.

Her sister gave a half-hearted wave, but then her head popped up. "You'll be gone the whole night?"

"Yup. So, don't go blowing anything up, because I won't be standing by with the fire extinguisher."

Galia rolled her eyes. "Any idea of when I'm going to meet this paramour of yours? You've been staying over a lot more, which must mean it's serious."

"Well..." Betty paused. "Maybe..."

"I mean, I don't care if he has two heads or five eyes. Although I will judge you if it turns out to be Gerard." Galia smiled easily at her joke, but Betty had to force her own smile.

"I'll see," she said. "We're just waiting for the right time."

"Well, let him know that I'm a terrible cook, but would love to have him over some time."

Betty forced her smile wider and nodded. "I'll pass

along the message to *him*," she said before quickly saying goodbye and hurrying off.

She barely noticed anything on her way to Wendy's apartment, surprising herself when she realized she was standing in front of Wendy's door. Taking a breath, she smoothed her hair and knocked.

"It's open!" Wendy called out from the other side.

It was always open, but Betty still always knocked and waited for a response. She walked into the apartment and headed straight for Wendy, who was in the kitchen, looking through the cupboards. Betty walked up behind her and wrapped her arms around her, resting her forehead on Wendy's shoulder.

"I'm a wuss," Betty said sadly.

Wendy took hold of her hands and leaned her head on Betty's. "I refuse to believe that."

Taking in a deep breath, Betty held Wendy closer, enjoying the warmth of her body and breathing in her vanilla and coconut scent. She wished that the rest of her life could be as easy as this. After a few minutes, she loosened her grip and Wendy turned around to face her.

"Rough day?" Wendy asked, wrapping her arms around Betty's shoulders.

"Mostly fine. I got a lot of work finished on the journal."

"Well, that sounds good."

Betty leaned her forehead against Wendy's. "It's also hungry work. Have you found anything that might resemble a meal yet?"

Wendy smiled. "I've found a takeout menu for The Penguin's Monocle."

"Pad thai?"

"Pad thai."

The two smiled and Wendy gave her a quick kiss before breaking away to find her phone and order them some food.

Galia was determined to make the chandelier fall the best effect this theatre had ever seen. Her current plan was to hang the chandelier over the audience and let it drop straight down, so that when it fell everyone would think it was going to fall on them and crush them all. It was going to be brilliant.

Well, it would be brilliant if she could figure out a way for it to not actually hit the audience, and if she could figure out what it would do once it stopped falling. But that's what rehearsals were for—trial and error. She paused. Hopefully her sister was making the chandelier out of something that wouldn't shatter.

Her major problem was that she couldn't get gravity to bend to her will. Another problem was that she was having trouble concentrating because of the loud knocking sound in the hallway. At first it was merely an annoyance, but then it started getting louder—loud enough to pull her out of her work. And before she could get back in, it sounded again, and again. Galia sighed in annoyance. Putting down her pen, she frowned deeply. She hated being distracted.

Grabbing her mp3 player from her backpack, she stuck the earbuds in her ears and turned on some music, hoping to drown out the knocking. It was impossible to work under these conditions.

CHAPTER FOURTEEN

She was standing in a dark, empty hallway. In her left hand was a wrought-iron lantern with a candle inside, but the light coming from it was weak, and she was only able to make out a few feet in front of her. As she took small, tentative steps forward, the lantern's light illuminated nothing except for the bare earthen floor and the dark walls of the hallway. There were no doorways or windows or other objects to be seen. The air around her was chilled and slightly musty, like that of a tomb.

She turned around to see what was behind her, but there was only darkness, as if the hallway was falling away with each step she took. Even the dim light of her lantern couldn't penetrate it. She wondered what would happen if she tried to turn back. Would her foot find an earthen floor, or would it disappear into the darkness?

Facing forward, she continued to walk. She could hear a noise in the distance, something that grew louder as she approached. Was it singing? Was there another person at the other end of the hallway singing a slow, mournful tune?

Soon she came to the end of the tunnel, which contained a large black door. The music was coming from within, and as she reached for the handle she wondered who was behind it.

A loud sharp knock startled her and she jumped back. The edges around the door began to glow a deep red and she watched as a dark red liquid began to bleed down the front of the door, coating it and changing it to the dark crimson colour of the basement door.

Another knock—but this time it came from behind the door, causing it to shudder violently. A small cry escaped her lips as the lantern fell from her hand and she turned away, running into the darkness.

She could no longer see anything, but still she ran, desperate to escape the terrible thing she knew was waiting for her behind the door. The knocking increased in intensity until it felt like it was coming from everywhere. Putting her hands over her ears, she closed her eyes and screamed for it to stop.

When she opened her eyes, she was standing on the stage of the theatre, wearing a white, old-fashioned dress. The audience was empty, but she could feel eyes staring at her, watching her. Her heart was still racing, but she didn't move. She had no idea what she was supposed to do or what her invisible audience expected, so it felt safer to do nothing.

But then the knocking started up again, sharp and quick at first, but growing louder each time. As she looked out at the auditorium, she noticed something red gently glowing behind the last row. As the object took shape, she realized that it was the basement door, shuddering with each knock, as if it was going to blow off its hinges.

The knocking came faster and louder and though she placed her hands over her ears again, it was so loud that it felt like it was inside her head, rattling her skull.

"LEAVE ME ALONE!" she screamed, but the knocking wouldn't stop.

Wendy woke up with a start. Her heart was pounding in her chest, but there was enough light coming through the window for her to see that she was in her own bed, safe in her apartment, with Betty sound asleep beside her. Taking in a deep breath, Wendy tried to slow her heartbeat and calm down.

It had been a while since she'd had a full-fledged nightmare and she didn't miss the feeling. As a child, she used to have nightmares whenever she was feeling particularly nervous or anxious about something. Her parents used to brush them off, telling her that she had nothing to fear from dreams, but it was her maternal grandmother who helped her work through them. Her *aanaga* explained the importance of symbolism and meaning, and whenever Wendy had a nightmare, the two of them would talk through it, figuring out what it meant, until the nightmares went away.

Wendy felt a pang of sadness as she remembered those moments. Although her mother refused to acknowledge her Inuit heritage, her *aanaga* had secretly taught her about their culture. It had to be kept secret, otherwise Wendy knew that her mother would stop letting her visit, but that made it even more exciting. Wendy's grandfather had died shortly after her mother was born, and her *aanaga* never remarried. She was strong and independent, and although she respected her daughter's decision to blend in, she also respected Wendy's desire to learn everything. In her youth, Wendy often wished that she could live with her *aanaga* instead of her parents, but never said anything because she knew it wouldn't be allowed.

Since her *aanaga's* passing seven years ago, Wendy had lost the one person she most wanted to talk to; the person she felt spiritually connected to; the person who loved her—faults and all. That was when her relationship with her parents began to fracture.

Taking in a deep breath, Wendy stared at the ceiling and conjured up the memory of her *aanaga*. She told her about the nightmare, hoping that the memory would provide some help, but all she could hear was her voice saying: *You know what this means. Think about, make it real, and acknowledge it.*

The music behind the door seemed to be some strange version of "Angel of Music" and she'd ended up on the stage at the end, so it was obviously related to the show. Maybe it was symbolic of her nervousness about getting the part of Christine. The only problem was that she didn't feel very nervous anymore. Her first rehearsal had gone well, and she knew deep down that she could do this. Any nerves she still felt were no different than the ones she had before the variety shows. Frowning, she wondered if those parts of the dream actually meant nothing and were simply weird bits cobbled together from the past few days.

The most important part of the dream was the knocking, so it was obviously related to the sounds at the theatre. Was it possible that the knocking was no longer limited to the theatre and was now invading her dreams? No, it was more likely that what had happened earlier outside the costume room was still lingering in her subconscious. It wasn't bad enough that she was scaring herself during the day—now her unconscious mind had to get in on it.

Looking through the window, she saw that the sky was starting to lighten with the dawn. Beside her, Betty slept peacefully, undisturbed by the events within Wendy's head. Turning towards her, Wendy gently placed her hand over Betty's, feeling the warmth and comfort of her touch, and closed her eyes.

CHAPTER FIFTEEN

"Gerard, *pour la dernière fois*, we are not putting a spot-light on you in the catwalk."

"But how will the audience know that it is I, the Phantom, up there?"

Jim huffed and counted to ten under his breath while the rest of the room watched silently. Wendy wondered if Ari was going to interrupt and take control of the situation, but she could see by the look on their face that they were enjoying the moment. Considering how temperamental Jim could be, sometimes it felt good to watch him be tormented.

"The audience will know it is you, because they will know your voice," Jim said sternly, the wrinkles on his forehead standing out prominently against his bald head.

But Gerard still wasn't satisfied by this answer. He cupped his chin with one hand and thought about it for a few seconds. "Are you suggesting that the Phantom should have some kind of catchphrase?"

Wendy forced back a laugh and tried to keep her shoulders from shaking with amusement. Jim's face instantly turned red and she could almost see smoke coming out of his ears. Although Gerard had started this conversation earnestly, she knew that he was now being deliberately obtuse. Bowing her head, she tried to concentrate on the scene they were supposed to be doing, but she could see out of the corner of her eye that Vance was still watching Jim and Gerard with an expression on his face that was equal parts confusion and uncertainty.

They weren't supposed to be working on scene 9 today, but Gerard had felt that his opinion was needed on every single scene in the script. He simply couldn't be expected to move on to scene 12 without first discussing scene 9.

Jim pinched the bridge of his nose and closed his eyes. "I am saying that the audience will not be full of idiots, and that if you give your character a catchphrase then *je vais vous assassiner et laisser votre corps dans une poubelle.*"

Gerard put his hands up in surrender and sighed. "Fine, Jim. I will trust that the audience will be smart enough to recognize my dulcet tones. Now, shall we discuss the Phantom's motivation for being at the masquerade?"

Wendy thought that Jim's head was actually going to explode as his face turned from a tomato red to a deep crimson.

Ari cleared their throat, holding back a laugh. "Gerard, we'll discuss the masquerade tomorrow afternoon, as the rehearsal schedule indicated. For now, let's move on to scene 12, *danke.*"

Gerard nodded and opened his script to the appropriate scene. Everyone busied themselves as they waited for Jim to calm down enough to continue with rehearsal, which—considering the colour of his face—didn't take as long as expected.

For the rest of rehearsal Gerard behaved and there were no other incidents. Still, Wendy could tell that Jim was relieved once they'd finished the final scene, and when Ari signalled that rehearsal was over, he was the first one out the door.

Wendy gathered her things, but her day wasn't over yet. Instead of going home for lunch, she grabbed some fries at LiLi's and ate them in the back of the auditorium while going over her script. Normally she'd go down to the dressing room, but she wanted to stay as far away from the knocking sound as possible. Every time she'd gone to the lower level over the past couple of days, she could hear the strange knocking, low and sinister, almost as if it were teasing her, so she'd decided to avoid that part of the theatre as much as possible. As long as she was careful not to leave a mess, she knew Ari wouldn't mind her eating in the auditorium.

As much as she tried to keep her mind off morbid things, she couldn't help looking around the room, remembering all the ghosts that Stacey had mentioned. There had been more than a few deaths in this area, and yet lately she only heard the knocking in the lower level. Her eyes moved over the empty seats, up the walls, to the darkness above, where the lighting grid was. Perhaps the knocking wasn't caused by one of the people who died in this room. Maybe it was someone who'd died on the lower level. Thinking back, she recalled Stacey saying that there was one actor who'd killed themselves in their dressing room, and a second who'd been killed by another actor. Unfortunately, Stacey hadn't elaborated on those incidents, so the first could have happened in the backstage or downstairs dressing rooms, and the second could have happened anywhere.

Munching absentmindedly on her fries, she thought back to what her *aanaga* had told her. There were two kinds of spirits: those who had unfinished business and couldn't let go of the material world, and those who wanted to cause pain and suffering. Was it possible that there was a spirit in the theatre who couldn't let go? Maybe that person had died during a production of "Phantom" and now that they were doing a similar show, it had re-awakened. Maybe all they needed to do was figure out what the ghost wanted and then it would leave them alone.

And yet, there was something about the knocking that made her think it wasn't as simple as that. What if it was the second kind of ghost? What if it was knocking to torment them, to make them feel scared? But why was it here now? And how could they get rid of it? What if it didn't want to go?

Giving herself a shake, she tried to clear her mind of all uncertainty and focus on her upcoming music rehearsal. Although there'd been no nightmare last night or the night before, this line of thinking would assure she'd have one tonight.

Finally, it was time to head up to the rehearsal hall again. This time it was only Ari and Rhonda, as Jim had other things to do. Wendy wondered if those other things happened to be avoiding Gerard for the next few hours while secretly plotting his death. Although Gerard wasn't here yet, Wendy had a feeling that he'd take this rehearsal more seriously.

When he showed up, Rhonda led them through a quick warm-up and then they sang "The Point of No

Return." They didn't have to do any acting or blocking, which made it easier to concentrate on getting the right notes.

They sang through it a few times, with Rhonda making corrections and adjustments. Then Gerard left and it was time for Wendy to work on "Think of Me." After that song, Francesca arrived and Rhonda talked to them about the songs she'd created for the opera within the show. Rhonda didn't bother leading Francesca through a warm-up, rightfully assuming that she'd warmed up at home.

Wendy knew nothing about *Faust*, but she was glad that Rhonda had created something that was in English and was more in line with the other songs they were singing. She had no idea how close it was to the actual opera but took Rhonda's word that it was quite similar.

When they finished the musical rehearsal, Wendy couldn't wait to get home and relax. They were only four days into rehearsal, but this show was much more involved than any other show they'd done. While Jim usually made the plays simpler, in order to fit within their small budget, he'd gone all out for this one. No wonder most of the designers looked haggard.

"You're doing fabulous, dear," Francesca said as they headed out of the theatre.

"Thanks," Wendy smiled. She had a feeling that she was doing okay, but it always helped to have someone else verify it. "I had no idea Jim was going to be so intense about this script. I mean, he wrote it, sure, but I've never seen him so particular about every little thing."

Francesca gave a bitter laugh. "He's always loved this story. He directed me in it a year before leaving Paris. Probably thought he'd never get to do it again."

Wendy nodded, and when she didn't say anything else, Francesca began to talk about the terribly conceited woman who'd played Carlotta in that production, and how much of a nightmare she was to work it. Wendy was thankful for the subject change. Sometimes she forgot that whenever she mentioned Jim she was talking about Francesca's ex-husband. There were decades of experiences shared between the two of them, but a sourness had tainted the memories, leaving them both with bitter tastes in their mouths. Although they tried to play nice in front of the rest of the troupe, at times it was impossible to ignore the past that weighed them both down like shackles.

It had taken some time, and many bottles of French wine, but eventually Wendy learned about the circumstances that brought Jim and Francesca to Jacobi Street.

Francesca Pettit had been a big star in Paris, acting in more plays than Wendy could name. She'd started out as a child actor, quickly becoming a theatre darling with her brilliant smile and sweet attitude, and the roles never stopped coming. Theatre soon became her life, and directors fell over themselves trying to cast her in their productions.

And then Jim Le Faull came along. When they met, he was also at the height of his fame as a talented director, and once Francesca caught his eye there was nothing that could turn his gaze away. Francesca was in her early twenties and Jim was seven years older than her, but the two quickly hit it off. Jim lavished her with gifts and prime theatrical roles, giving her everything her heart desired, and they dated for two years before marrying. For almost a decade they were a theatrical power couple, dominating the Parisian theatre scene.

But then came the fall. Over time, people became suspicious of Jim's ability to always be able to afford whatever he needed for a show, no matter the cost, and a small group of rivals began to dig into his business practices. They soon realized that Jim's covert business partners were not only involved in distasteful business practices—such as arson, blackmail, and smuggling—but that they may also have been responsible for the downfall of many others within the theatrical community—others who threatened Jim's rise to the top.

Jim swore to Francesca that he knew nothing about his backers' terrible business dealings, and at that time she had no reason to think he would lie. But even if he was innocent, the speculation was out there and the damage was done. Since Jim was unable to prove his innocence, it was decided that the best thing for them to do would be to leave Paris and lie low for a few years, until the whole thing blew over. Francesca didn't want to give up her home or her life, but her husband assured her that all they needed were a few months or maybe a year away, and then they'd be able to return to their normal lives.

Jim moved them all the way across the Atlantic Ocean. He purchased a small theatre and called it *Le Petit Paris*, managing to give them a home and a place to work in this strange new city. Although Francesca found the street charming, the body of work that the theatre did was less than desirable, and the small apartment on the third floor only reminded her of how far she'd fallen. Not only was she thousands of miles away from her home and friends, but she had been reduced to performing bare-bones theatre for nearly empty houses. She was certain she'd end up working as a waitress within a year.

But then Jim's magical ability to find money came through. In less than a year, he found the theatre a benefactor with more money than brains, but the money came with a catch. This man loved old vaudeville theatres and variety shows and only agreed to give Jim money if he promised to put on a bi-monthly variety show for him. If Jim did that, the theatre would have enough money to hire full-time actors and crew, and even a little left over to put on an actual show once a month.

While Francesca regarded this as a giant leap backwards in her career, she tried to look on the bright side. Performing in the variety show gave her a chance to explore different characters, and she was still with Jim and in love. They hired more actors and designers, and the theatre seemed to spring to life. Some days, if she closed her eyes and added a few embellishments, it was almost like the good old days.

But no matter how good things got, she still longed for home. After two years on Jacobi Street, she asked Jim about returning, but he said that it wasn't time yet and they needed to wait longer. Every year after, she'd asked him about going home, and every year he'd say no; they needed more time. After a while she felt as if she would never get home. She stopped following her rigid diet, stopped practising her talents every day, and fell into a dark mood. After ten years of their self-imposed exile had passed, she told Jim that he had ruined her life, that she would never see Paris again because of him, and that she wanted a divorce.

On the day she moved out, Jim rechristened *Le Petit Paris* as The Quaint Little Theatre.

CHAPTER SIXTEEN

"I just had a brilliant idea!"

Betty looked up from the mask she was painting with an expression of alarm on her face. It was never a good thing when her sister had brilliant ideas. Great ideas and awesome ideas were okay, but brilliant ideas usually resulted in hospital trips.

"What is it?" Betty asked cautiously.

Galia was standing in the doorway of the props room, a large, insane smile on her face. "What if we let the chandelier actually fall on the audience?" She opened her arms wide, expecting an enthusiastic response, but Betty's mind was too busy trying to work through all the health and safety issues with that idea to respond. Eventually Galia put her arms on her hips and stared at her sister.

"Wouldn't that be... dangerous?" Betty finally managed to say.

"You're not thinking about it the right way," Galia said, walking over to her. "We kill a few seats in the house, the ones directly underneath the chandelier, so that when it falls it doesn't hit anyone. The chandelier would have to be smaller, and we'd have to move it to the front of the audience so that everyone sees it, but wouldn't it be so cool to have the chandelier *actually* fall? I mean, what other theatre has the guts to do something like that!?"

Betty wanted to say that it wasn't guts that stopped other companies from doing such a thing, it was more like insurance and liability, but she refrained. "Are you sure Jim would be okay with not selling a portion of the audience? You know that sometimes a lot of people come to our shows."

Galia waved her hand dismissively. "When Jim hears about this idea, he's going to have to add extra performances!"

"I mean, you'll have to run it past Ari first," Betty said, thankful that she could hide behind the stage manager. If Ari said no then Galia would have to let it go, and if Ari said yes then it meant there was a safe way to do the stunt.

"I'm sure Ari will see reason. I mean, they know a brilliant idea when they hear it."

Betty nodded. "Well, whatever happens, let me know ASAP. If I have to change the design of the chandelier so that it's foam instead of wood or plastic, I'll have to know soon."

"Foam?" Galia laughed maniacally. "If we're going to drop this sucker, I don't want to hear a soft 'thud'—I want a *crash*!"

And that was it—the moment that Betty realized she would do just about anything to not have this effect approved. Maybe she could text Ari to warn them... or bribe them to say no...

"You're ridiculous, sis. Have I ever told you that?" Galia laughed the entire way out of the room.

"I'm worried that Galia's going to kill the audience," Betty said as she stepped into Wendy's apartment.

Wendy had been lying on the couch, but at Betty's words she lifted her head up and looked in Betty's direction. "How is this different than any other show we've worked on?" she asked.

Betty crossed to the couch and leaned over the back, looking down at her. "On the other shows I'm usually worried that she's going to kill herself or one of the actors. This time I'm worried she's going to take out half the audience."

Wendy sat up and gave Betty her full attention. "What's she doing now?"

Sighing deeply, Betty filled her in on Galia's 'brilliant' plan to drop the chandelier on the audience. By the end, Wendy's eyes were wide with surprise.

"Ari wouldn't let her," Wendy said. "I mean, she'll end up killing someone. If not with the drop, then maybe with shrapnel."

"I know." Betty sighed again. "I really hope that Ari says no."

Wendy gave her a reassuring smile. "Ari's smart. They'll say no. I mean, it's not like we need any more ghosts at the theatre."

A quizzical look crossed Betty's face. "More ghosts? What does that mean?"

Wendy realized what she'd just said. "Nothing, I just..." She paused. "Stacey started it. Well, the knocking started it. You know that knocking from the furnace?"

Betty nodded. "Francesca said something about it last week."

"Well, Stacey said it's probably a ghost trying to communicate with us, and then went and dug up a bunch of stories about people who died in the theatre."

"Huh..." Betty's brows furrowed. "But it's just the furnace knocking. Why would she think it was a ghost?"

Wendy shrugged. "According to Stacey, any theatre worth its salt has a ghost hanging around. Francesca tried to tell her that there weren't any ghosts here, but Stacey latched onto the idea and ran with it."

"Someone really needs to tell her that ghosts aren't real," Betty said, shaking her head.

Her voice was so matter-of-fact that Wendy suddenly felt ashamed for her earlier thoughts about spirits. The feeling went away quickly, but it was there long enough for Betty to notice.

"Oh no, did I say something wrong?" Betty's face fell. "I don't mean to say that you're wrong if you believe in ghosts. I might be wrong. Maybe ghosts really do exist."

Her sincerity was almost enough to make Wendy laugh, but instead she smiled and placed her hand on Betty's. "It's okay. My grandmother taught me to believe in spirits, so although I've never seen one, I'm open to the idea. But I don't think there's a ghost at the theatre." She paused. Her resolve wavered as the memory of the sinister knocking loomed in the back of her mind, and a frown crossed her face.

"Wait," Betty said, moving around the couch so that she could sit down next to Wendy. "Do you think there might be a ghost in the theatre?"

Cursing her face for being so easy to read, Wendy figured that it would be best to be honest. "I don't know, but I get a really creepy feeling about the knocking. Sometimes it's low, sometimes it's loud, and sometimes it's enough to split to my head open. If it were consistent then maybe I'd think otherwise, but it almost seems to have a mind of its own. There's something that's just... not natural about it."

Although she'd thought this numerous times in her head, it was strange to say the words out loud. Wendy half-expected Betty to make fun of her superstitious ideas, but instead she nodded.

"That does sound weird. I can't say I've had the same experience, but I tend to zone out when I'm working, so I haven't really heard any knocking. And even if I had, I'd think it was the furnace." Her face suddenly went serious as she reached forward and took Wendy's hand in hers. "However, if you plan on trying to confront this ghost and you need a non-believer to hold your hand, I'll be there." She winked and smiled.

Wendy burst out laughing. "I'll be sure to remember that."

CHAPTER SEVENTEEN

Rehearsals for the rest of the week went well, with most of the show getting blocked except for the four big crowd scenes. Everyone gathered on Thursday afternoon to read through the scenes and ask any questions they might have, so that Jim could devote all of Friday and Saturday to blocking and choreography. Almost every actor was involved in the scenes, which meant that everyone was going to have a couple of very long days. Even the designers were expected to attend, so that they'd have a better idea of what those moments would look like and, possibly, to fill in as extras.

Group scenes were always harder to block because there were so many moving pieces, and it didn't help that Jim was so exacting with his ideas. Friday morning was scheduled for the opening gala for the new manager, and the afternoon was for the masquerade where the Phantom makes an appearance. Then on Saturday they'd take on the performance at the Opera House where the chandelier falls, and the performance where the Phantom abducts Christine.

By this point they had all the "stand in" set pieces,

which they'd use until the actual set pieces were ready or until they finally started rehearsing on the stage. They also had a number of "stand in" props to use, like letters and swords. Their costumes were still being worked on, but Paloma had provided certain actors with a few basic costume pieces to help with spacing and characterization—vests or pants for the male characters, and full skirts for the characters performing within the Opera House.

As Wendy pulled her rehearsal skirt on over her jeans, she told herself that today was too important to mess around. It could be awfully easy to become distracted or lost in thought while Jim was working on a part of a scene she wasn't needed in. As a lead character, it'd be best for her to set an example, like Francesca did, and be on her best behaviour.

Jim and Ari were sitting at the table along the back wall, but seats had been put out on either side for the designers, so that they could get a good view of what was going on. The only exceptions were Rhonda, who sat at the piano in the stage-right corner, and Scott, who was sitting in a chair that had been pushed back into the far corner of stage-left, his head ducked low over his clipboard, as if trying to avoid being noticed. As Wendy took in the designers, she noticed how tired most of them seemed.

Once everyone had arrived and was ready to rehearse, Jim got down to business. The opening scene didn't involve much choreography, as most of the characters stayed in small groups, celebrating the new manager of the Opera House, and gossiping about theatre business. The crowds parted to the sides as Christine came on stage to perform in place of Carlotta, who turned down the opportunity in a fit of ego. After Christine was mobbed by her adoring fans, she withdrew from the stage, and Raoul, having recognized her, followed. The party continued until Stacey burst on as Jammes, a ballerina who'd spotted the Phantom near the dressing rooms. There was a moment of panic, which would be increased by the special effect of a body dropping from the ceiling, sending the scene into total chaos. Although they couldn't drop the body in this room, Ari described the effect to everyone, giving them a cue when it was supposed to happen.

Wendy found herself thinking back to Stacey's stories about the director who'd hung himself and the stagehand who'd fallen from the lighting grid. She tried to remind herself that those spirits seemed to be gone and hoped that they'd made peace with their deaths. She didn't want any more of them waking up because of this show.

Billy and Betty were expected to be extra characters on stage, to make the party look more full. When Jim mentioned that one of them would have to say a line, Betty's eyes had widened in fear, so Billy stepped forward and said he'd do it, earning a grateful look from Betty.

Within two and a half hours, they'd finished blocking the first scene and had run it a couple times (skipping over the song for now). After a short break, Jim quickly moved on to the masquerade, which he knew would take longer because it involved choreography. There wasn't much dialogue, but Jim wanted a grand song and dance to start the scene. It involved all the actors, except for Wendy, who would enter shortly after the dance ended. There were a few moments of Jim muttering about how in the old days he'd have a professional choreographer to work with, but

Wendy could see that he enjoyed creating the dance, even if he found some of the actors less than ideal to work with. As she watched, Wendy imagined what it must be like to work in a theatre where you could have twenty or thirty actors, all dancing together on a large stage. She liked her little troupe but couldn't help picturing how spectacular this show would be if Jim had been able to hire twice as many people to work on it.

Since there were no special effects in the scene, Galia had been roped into being a background body with Billy and Betty. They didn't have to dance or sing, but they'd get to wear costumes and masks and move about to "fill the space."

The dance took almost an hour to instruct, mainly because of Samuel's two left feet, Vance's being new to this kind of dancing, and Gerard spending most of his time looking at Carina instead of his dancing partner, Francesca. Wendy was determined not to grow bored or impatient, and spent the time going over her lines while sitting in the area of the room that had been designated as the off-right wing.

When it was time for her to enter the scene, she was excited at the opportunity to finally do something. The dance partners changed up as Raoul moved over to join her, and Gerard went backstage to prepare for his next entrance as the Phantom. Jim had those who were still onstage perform a much simpler dance, but there was a lot of careful blocking that needed to be done, so that nobody ran into anyone else. With so many people on stage, and Christine and Raoul trying to have a private conversation, there were a lot of things to focus on.

They hadn't yet made it to the end of the scene before it was time to break for dinner. Wendy, Stacey, and Carina decided to go to Curds & Whey, a local street vendor who specialized in tofu and vegetables. They were all hungry enough to eat a horse but knew that the healthier alternative would keep them from wanting to take a nap during the rest of rehearsal.

Before everyone knew it, it was time to start up again. Jim finally finished blocking the masquerade, and then had them run through the scene a few times, before going back to the opening scene.

By the time rehearsal ended, everyone was exhausted. And they all knew that there was still one more long day to go.

CHAPTER EIGHTEEN

After rehearsal was over, Carina caught Gerard's eye, huffed, and turned away. She quickly gathered her things and headed downstairs, not exiting at the stage level like everyone else, but going all the way to the lower level. She walked into Sam and Gerard's dressing room, knowing that it was less likely for Sam to show up in there than for Wendy or Stacey to show up in the room the girls shared.

Although they rarely used the dressing rooms during a show's rehearsal period, it still smelled like Sam's cologne—which she referred to as "old man smell." Carina wrinkled her nose and lifted herself up to sit on the counter, being careful not to sit too far back because of the lightbulbs framing the mirrors. While she waited for Gerard, she looked around the room, which was mostly empty. There were no costumes hanging in the racks on the other side of the room, and other than a few skincare odds and ends that Gerard kept on his side of the counter, the space was quite empty. The girls usually kept their stage makeup in their dressing room, so they didn't have to keep trucking it back and forth between shows, which made their room look much more cluttered. At least it smelled better.

Voices on the other side of the door let her know that some of the designers were in the hallway—likely going to their offices to get some more work done before calling it a night. She crossed her arms and let out an angry sigh, hoping that Gerard had gotten the message. Tomorrow was going to be another long day, and she didn't want to waste most of her night waiting for him to show up. Thankfully, less than a minute later, Gerard walked into the room.

"Carina..." he said, rolling the "r" and putting as much seduction into her name as the three syllables would allow. "Why have you been so distant lately?"

She pouted and turned her head away from him. "You promised me that you would get me the lead role in *Phantom*. Yet here I am, having to play an old woman." She said the last two words as if they were the saddest words in the English language.

Gerard walked closer, stopping in front of her. "Darling, I talked to Jim, but he was worried that your beauty would distract from the story." A smile played along his lips. "How could I not agree with such an indisputable observation?"

She huffed again, but in a haughtier manner, turning her head in a way that elongated her neck. "You said that last time..." she pouted, pushing out her lower lip.

"Because it was true last time, as well." He gently laid a hand on her face and she allowed him to turn her head back to him. "Carina... my *querida*. You know I'm your biggest fan."

She pouted again, but there was a glint of a smile in her brown eyes. Gerard only spoke Spanish when there was a particular activity on his mind.

He placed his other hand on the other side of her face. "Do you forgive me?"

"This time," she said before leaning in for a kiss. Eventually he lowered his hands, moving them down her body until they rested on her thighs.

She pulled away. "Not here."

Less than a minute later, they were in the basement, tucked away behind a pile of rarely used set pieces in the far back corner. It wasn't their favourite place to fool around within the theatre, but with so many people still wandering the building, it was the least likely place for anyone to walk in on them.

Carina let out a soft moan as Gerard slipped his hands under her shirt, sliding them up to her chest. Yes, she was disappointed that she hadn't gotten the part of Christine, but the truth was that she'd figured out how useless Gerard was a long time ago. He only cared about one thing — himself. His focus was getting himself a good part, and with Sam as his only competition, it meant he basically had to do nothing but continue dying his hair and working out. Sure, he would try to convince her that he'd spoken to Jim about giving her better parts, but she knew that he was lying.

The whole situation was folly on her part. Five months after joining the troupe, she'd decided that the only way to get better parts was to seduce someone important and convince them that it'd be a great idea to cast her in the lead roles. Setting her sights on their resident leading man, Gerard, she began to pursue him. It had been much easier than she'd originally thought, and the fact that Gerard was a self-serving narcissist made her feel much less guilty about using him. Getting the lead roles, however, wasn't as simple.

She could have called off this useless charade many times, but the truth was that she needed an excuse to see him and this was better than anything else she could come up with. As much as she hated to admit it, Gerard was one of the best sexual partners she'd ever had—not that she'd ever tell him. His ego was large enough for now, and she sure as hell wasn't going to be the reason it increased.

There weren't a lot of eligible bachelors around these parts, and it was helpful to have someone she could call if she ever got an itch. She'd thrown a few advances at Vance, hoping to hook the newcomer with her charms, but he seemed to be made of ice. Meanwhile, every time she threw an advance at Gerard, he was more than ready to catch it.

Pulling him closer, she kissed him deeply, closing her eyes and picturing Vance's face instead of his. Her smile spread wider as one of his hands travelled down her thigh and between her legs, but her thoughts were quickly interrupted by a loud knock. She jumped and let out a startled cry.

"It's just the pipes," Gerard said, trailing kisses down her neck.

Laughing it off, she closed her eyes and arched her body towards him. He let out a low moan and quickly reached for his belt, undoing his pants.

When the next knock sounded, they were too involved to notice. They didn't notice the one after that, or the next one, or the next. And when the lights in the basement started to take on a deep red glow and the shadows began to rise around them, it was already too late.

CHAPTER NINETEEN

Saturday's rehearsal seemed easier than Friday's, although Wendy wasn't sure if that was because they'd already been through one gruelling day or if it was because there weren't as many bodies on stage at the same time.

First, they worked on the scene where the chandelier falls, which was the final scene of Act 1. It took place during a performance of *Faust*, and some characters were watching the show, while others were performing the play within a play. Before the show, the Phantom had tried to scare Carlotta from performing, but ended up only making her more determined to go onstage. Meanwhile, Christine was distracted because she was torn between the Phantom and Raoul; she's unable to escape the Phantom and doesn't want to involve Raoul in her difficult situation, but she's also unable to ignore her heart and turn Raoul away. The new owner of the theatre and his aide, Moncharmin and Remy, are watching the opera from the infamous Box 5, with Moncharmin eager to prove that this Phantom business is all nonsense, while Raoul watches from another Box.

The scene started with a short dance by Meg, as a kind

of introduction to the opera. Then Meg left and Christine came on stage to sing. This scene took place right after the one where Carlotta accused Christine of using the Phantom to try and scare her away from performing. Shortly after Carlotta's departure, Raoul appeared and a fight ensued about the Phantom, so Christine's emotions were quite high as she stepped onto the stage.

Jim informed Wendy that Christine would try to sing well at first, but then her resolve would falter, and her performance would suffer. Afterwards, she'd step into the background and Carlotta would come on stage to great applause and begin singing. But Carlotta's joy would be short-lived as the Phantom had other plans, taunting her from above. The scene ended with the chandelier falling from the sky, interrupting the opera and bringing the show into intermission.

As Ari described how the chandelier would drop from the ceiling before being caught on a safety line, Wendy glanced over at Galia, who was trying to hide her frown. She was quite thankful that Galia's insane idea to actually drop the chandelier on the audience had been vetoed.

Other than Carina's choreography, the scene was quite easy to block, and they quickly moved on to the final group scene, which took place during the Opera's performance of *Don Juan*. It was the performance between Christine and the Phantom, although nobody was supposed to know that it was the Phantom until his cover was blown.

First there was a dance by Jammes and Meg, and after that Christine would come onstage to start "The Point of No Return." The Phantom would join her, in disguise, and she wasn't supposed to realize that her scene partner was actually the Phantom until his voice began to sound familiar to her, about two-thirds through the song. At the end of the song, she would rip off the Phantom's mask, revealing his scarred face, and then the lights would go down. When the lights came back up, she and the Phantom would be gone, and a knife would be driven into the stage where they had been standing.

After the blocking had been figured out, Jim had them rehearse the scenes a few times. Then there was enough time to go through Friday's scenes again, to help cement them into everyone's brains.

By the time rehearsal ended on Saturday, they had officially blocked the entire show. Wendy wondered if this was what it felt like to scale Mount Everest. She had no idea what the scenes she wasn't in looked like, but if they were anything like hers, then this was going to be a show to remember. They still had to add in costumes and sets, but even without them Jim had managed to outdo himself. It was amazing what the team had accomplished so far.

Before everyone left, Jim handed out the scripts and cast list for next week's variety show. Even though tomorrow was a day off, everyone knew that Jim would expect them to spend part of the day learning lines for the variety show and the other part learning lines for *Phantom*. Wendy was glad that this week-long overlap only happened once a month.

"Supper?" Stacey asked, as she gathered her stuff. Carina and Wendy nodded emphatically. They headed to The Belle Verde, managing to grab the last empty booth seat in the half-crowded restaurant.

"Well, that was fun," Stacey said as she took a long sip of the beer Gradey had quickly placed in front of her. He had noticed the exhausted looks on their faces and fetched their drinks faster than usual. "We need to stop doing group scenes. Like, forever."

"At least it was easier than yesterday," Wendy said. "That masquerade dance at the top of the scene is insane."

Carina nodded. "You should be thankful you only have to learn the easier one."

"I am," Wendy replied honestly.

Stacey's eyes narrowed. "How's it working with Vance? You cracked that nut yet?"

Wendy wasn't sure what Stacey was asking but was pretty sure it was lewd. "He's okay. I mean, we don't really talk that much outside of rehearsal, but he's not a jerk. And he's a good actor."

"He's extremely cold," Carina added, stifling a yawn. "But still definitely hot."

Stacey raised an eyebrow. "Oh, is someone tired today? Perhaps had a late night yesterday?"

"I am an adult and will do what I wish," Carina shot back.

Stacey turned to Wendy and gave her a knowing look. "She didn't get in until after 2am," she stage-whispered, making sure her voice was loud enough for Carina to hear. Carina glared at her.

Wendy smiled, but didn't say anything. She'd noticed the dark circles under Carina's eyes and knew that the most likely answer was that Carina had been out late with Gerard, and she didn't want to think about that before eating. It was bad enough that her nightmare had come back last night—she didn't want to risk thinking about things that might give her different nightmares.

Before Stacey could say anything else, Gradey arrived with their food.

"Has anyone heard any knocking from the furnace lately?" Stacey said as they all tucked in.

Wendy paused, trying to figure out if she should admit to hearing the knocking and how strange it was, or if it was better to keep quiet and not encourage Stacey.

"I heard it the other day," Carina said flippantly.

"Excellent," Stacey nodded, her hand hovering over the chips on her plate. "That means the ghost is still in the theatre and is still trying to communicate with us!"

Carina laughed. "No, it means that Jim's still too cheap to hire someone to look at the furnace."

Rolling her eyes, Stacey picked up a chip and popped it in her mouth. "It means that the ghost is still around and that we should hold a séance to try and communicate with it."

Carina laughed out loud as Wendy shook her head.

"Come on," Stacey pleaded. "I don't want to do it alone, and you're my best hope. I've got the Ouija board and everything. We just need to pick a night."

"My grandmother taught me not to mess with spirits," Wendy said, tucking into her food and hoping that Stacey would let the subject drop.

Stacey turned her gaze to Carina, pleading.

Carina shook her head. "I've got better things to do with my life, *querida*."

"You two are the worst," Stacey muttered.

CHAPTER TWENTY

Galia stomped down to the special effects room, all the while muttering about being surrounded by philistines. Betty was close at her heels, sensing her sister's mood and knowing that she'd need to be calmed down.

"Plan B is just fine," Betty said gently, trying to sound upbeat.

Galia gave her a stern look. She'd tried three times to communicate how amazing her idea was and why it would be the best idea ever, but each time she was told that it was too risky and would take too many seats out of commission. After rehearsal she'd tried for a fourth, knowing that their current plan was way too simple, but she'd been shut down by Ari before she could even open her mouth

Betty knew that eventually she'd get over it, but left to her own devices, Galia would grumble for weeks instead of hours, and with a show this elaborate, they didn't have time for that kind of tantrum.

"Plan B is fine if you like *boring*," Galia shot back. "I mean, any theatre can make a chandelier look like it's falling, but we could've had the most amazing effect *ever*.

I mean, it's not like we ever sell out a performance, so what's wrong with killing a few rows? We even could've put a dummy in the row, and that could've been the person who gets the chandelier dropped on their head, and then medics could come in, and it would be totally immersive…"

Sighing, Betty tried to think of what she could say to get Galia's head back in her work. The chandelier was never going to drop at all if she didn't start working on it soon. They had fewer than two weeks before the show opened, and they still had a variety show to prep and perform. Maybe she could distract her with another effect to work on, but that wouldn't solve the problem. Galia needed her interest in the chandelier renewed and reinvigorated.

Looking out into the hallway, Betty noticed Billy walking past. "Hey, Billy!" she called out. "What do you think about the catch line for the chandelier being lower?"

Billy paused and turned around, and when Betty saw the exhausted look on his face, she felt guilty for disturbing him. She opened her mouth to apologize, but he interrupted her.

"Depends on how low you're talking about," he said, walking into the room. He leaned heavily against the doorway, but otherwise seemed mentally alert. "How much more of a drop are you thinking?"

Betty glanced over at Galia, who was muttering quietly to herself, and raised her voice. "What about four feet above the audience? That'll give most of the audience time to notice it and look up."

Billy absently stroked his beard with one hand. "I don't know. It might be too risky. What if someone stands up?"

"Good point." She paused to think. "How else can we make sure that everyone notices the drop? The current set-up's pretty quick."

"What if we had it swing down and towards the stage? We could use a catch line before it reaches the stage, perhaps shut the curtains as it swings, just in case anything flies off?"

"It's supposed to fall *on* the audience!" Galia turned on them angrily, standing with her hands on her hips and giving them a look that suggested their idea was beyond stupid.

"I know," Billy replied gently, "but if we injure a patron, even by accident, we're all going to be out of a job."

Galia opened her mouth to argue, but then shut it again. Betty and Billy waited patiently as she frowned, tilted her head, frowned harder, and then stared up at the ceiling. Billy started to speak, but Betty put a hand on his arm and shook her head.

"Okay, new plan!" Galia said. "We hang the chandelier over audience centre. When the Phantom finishes doing his thing, we let off a few fireworks—*harmless* fireworks," she added after seeing a look of alarm cross Betty's face. "The chandelier drops and swings down towards the stage, the lights go out, the chandelier swings into the stage, curtains close, lights back on, and then we remove the chandelier during intermission?"

Betty thought over the plan. Then she thought about it a second time. It sounded... reasonable. "The fireworks would draw the audience's attention... I like the idea of making it 'disappear' with the lights going down, and it

would be easier to clear away if it's on the stage at intermission."

"Sounds good," Billy nodded. He suppressed a yawn.
"I can help you with some of the details if you need."

Galia nodded. "I've got a few things to figure out first,
but I'll let you know what I come up with. Then you two
can help me convince Jim and Ari that this is the best idea
ever." Moving over to her drafting table, Galia picked up
a pen and started scribbling.

Billy and Betty exchanged a look and exited the room,
leaving Galia alone with her work.

"Thank you for that," Betty said softly as they walked
down the hall.

"Anytime," Billy smiled, but the smile didn't quite
reach his eyes.

"Hey, are you sleeping okay?" Betty asked. "You seem
tired."

He shook his head. "It must be something in the air.
I'm sure it's nothing."

"Well, take care of yourself. Spend your day off relax-
ing. I don't know what this theatre would do without you,
so don't get sick, okay?" she teased, smiling at him.

He gave her a big smile. "I'll do my best."

But as he walked away, Betty couldn't help worrying
that there was something Billy wasn't telling her.

CHAPTER TWENTY-ONE

Jim had been drinking steadily since mid-afternoon. Although rehearsals for *Phantom* were going about as well could be expected, there was still so much more that needed to be done. He didn't just want this show to be perfect, he *needed* it to be. If he could show Lodge how a real show looked, then maybe he'd be able to squeeze some more money out of the old fogey and finally get this theatre operating at its full potential.

Stumbling down the private stairs from his apartment and into the lobby, he wondered if there was any alcohol hiding around the theatre. He'd just finished his last bottle of scotch and didn't want to leave the building to buy more. Inebriation of this level was best kept to oneself and one's best friends—if such things were possible to have. He should have restocked days ago, but rehearsals had been taking up so much of his time.

The theatre was empty and dark, with the ghost light shining brightly on the stage. Although he preferred for a theatre to be full of people and movement, over the years he'd come to appreciate the quieter moments. Perhaps it had something to do with the current company he'd gathered. In the old days nobody would have dared talk back to him, and if he gave an order it would be followed to the letter. *Merde*, he needed a drink.

Ari probably had a multitude of spirits pocketed around the booth, but he'd bet they were too well-hidden. Even though he'd owned the theatre for sixteen years and Ari had only been hired seven years ago, Ari knew more of the building's secrets than he did. If he cared about things like that, it might bother him, but he didn't. Besides, taking Ari's secret alcohol wouldn't be worth the trouble that he'd get if they found out, so there was no point in trying. Billy never drank at the theatre, and although Jim wasn't sure if Betty drank, he figured she must not because she'd be a lot more relaxed if she did. He hoped that Galia didn't drink at the theatre, because she was unstable enough sober, although it would explain a few things. So that left Paloma...

Wandering through the empty auditorium, Jim brought up a vague memory of Paloma pulling a bottle of something from behind her sewing machine. Hadn't she mentioned something about using vodka to clean costumes? Stumbling past the empty seats, he manoeuvred to the backstage area, using the ghost light to guide his way. It was late Sunday evening and although a few designers had come in during the day to work, they were long gone by now. There was nobody to disturb him in his quest.

He muttered to himself as he made his way to the lower level. When he moved to this godforsaken city, he'd intended to spend a few years here before returning to Paris, but it turned out that while he was away even more dirty laundry had been aired. He never told Francesca about these new revelations, or how it was likely that he'd never be able to show his face in Europe ever again. He'd die in this damned city, his name tainted by his own ambition.

And Francesca... Perhaps it had been selfish to insist that she come with him, but he couldn't imagine starting over on his own. He couldn't blame her for eventually leaving him—he only wished that he'd been brave enough to be honest with her about everything. Instead, they were trapped in this quaint little purgatory, never rising further, yet never falling.

When he reached Paloma's office, he was careful not to disturb too much, and to right anything that he accidentally knocked over. It took a bit of searching, but eventually he discovered a bottle of white rum tucked behind the serger. Smiling to himself, he took a long drink from the bottle and left the office.

He'd have one hell of a hangover tomorrow, but right now all he wanted to do was drink more to numb the pain. This theatre was making him feel like Sisyphus—working so hard to reach the top only to have to start over at the bottom again and again. If he could get more money or another benefactor then he could hire someone else to deal with the variety show and spend his time working on real art, but it was almost impossible to make money in this city. People on this side of the world didn't care as much about the arts—especially when it came to the smaller theatres. Maybe it'd be better for him to give it all up and try again in a new city, but he'd doubt that his team would follow him, and he was getting too old to start over from scratch. Again.

Taking another swig, he tried to focus on *Fantôme* and

how wonderful it would be once everything came together. If he could pull this off, then it would prove that he'd always been an amazing director and visionary. If the right kind of people came to see the show, then he'd be one step closer to reclaiming his future.

Approaching the stairwell, he suddenly realized that the door to the basement was open. Turning and squinting at the door, he tried to remember if it had been open when he'd come downstairs. He was sure he'd have noticed if it had, but perhaps he'd been too drunk.

Walking over to the door to shut it, he noticed that there was a dull red light emanating from within. Peering into the room, he wondered if the alcohol was affecting his vision as the red glow began to pulse.

As if in a trance, the hand holding the bottle lowered to his side and Jim stepped into the basement.

CHAPTER TWENTY-TWO

She was standing on the stage of The Quaint Little Theatre. It was completely empty, with no set pieces, backdrops, or other people around. In front of her were rows of plush red seats, and even though there was nobody sitting in them, she could sense people out there, staring at her.

Squinting, she tried to make out any shapes or forms, but there was nothing except for that feeling of multiple eyes watching her from different areas of the room. Who were these people? Why couldn't she see them? Were they waiting for her to do something? Acting? Singing?

She wanted to leave the stage and get away from the invisible eyes, but it felt as if her feet were glued to the floor. She opened her mouth to speak, but didn't know what to say, so she closed it without a word. She didn't understand why she was here or what was going on.

A loud knock startled her. She turned to her head to the right, still unable to move her feet. Behind her she could see the door that led backstage, except it wasn't that door, it was the basement door. A red glow was around the edges, bleeding into the room. The knock happened again, shaking the door violently. As it happened again and again, growing louder each time, she realized that it sounded like it was moving closer.

A sudden chill gripped her and she wrapped her arms around herself. Something was coming—something bad. She couldn't see it and had no idea what it was but knew that it was evil.

The knocking grew louder as it approached; her eyes stayed fixed on the basement door. Fear enveloped her heart in an icy grip. What was coming? What did it want? Why wouldn't it leave her alone?

The feeling of being watched grew stronger and she wondered if this was what the audience was waiting for. Was this the show? Were they here to witness her demise? She wanted to turn and see if the audience had suddenly materialized, but her eyes refused to leave the basement door. Something inside told her that if she looked away, she'd regret it.

All she could do was stand and wait for whatever was coming. She could do nothing to stop it.

Wendy woke up with a start, her heart pounding loudly in her chest. Moonlight illuminated the room, letting her know that she was in her apartment, but she still pinched herself to ensure that she wasn't still asleep.

Turning on her side, she pulled the covers around her and tried to fight the chill that the nightmare had brought on. The dream had been so unsettling and fearful, but already it was starting to slip away, and the details were fading. She tried desperately to cling onto whatever she could—the theatre, unseen eyes watching her, and the evil coming towards her—but most of the details were gone within seconds.

Taking in a deep breath, she tried to tell herself that

it was just a dream. She'd been spending too much time thinking about ghosts and evil spirits, and now it was invading her dreams. It was merely her brain being overactive—too full of this nonsense to know what to do with it. It wasn't anything to be afraid of.

But what if it was? What if the dreams were trying to tell her something?

Wendy closed her eyes and tried to shake those kinds of thoughts out of her head. The theatre was safe, there were no ghosts, and it was simply her imagination blowing things out of proportion. It was stress—nothing more. Nothing more.

CHAPTER TWENTY-THREE

The next week at the theatre was a grim one. Everyone was feeling stressed and overworked, and many of them had dark circles under their eyes and yawned whenever they thought nobody was looking.

Although this wasn't the first time the troupe had rehearsed two shows at the same time, they'd never tried to pull off such an elaborate full-length show. To accommodate for this, Jim had simplified the variety show slightly—re-using some sets, having a few simpler skits, and giving the biggest parts to those who weren't as prominent in *Phantom*—but it was only barely less complicated than last week's show. He still needed it to be as detailed and interesting as it usually was; otherwise, they'd run the risk of annoying their benefactor and getting their support cut off.

As Wendy made her way to the downstairs dressing room on the night of the variety show, she noticed how haggard everyone was looking. There were a few people who didn't seem as affected by the amount of work piled on their shoulders, like Francesca and Ari, while everyone else ran the gamut from "exhausted" to "dead on their feet." Wendy wondered if there was some weird flu going around. Nobody was coughing or had a fever or had asked for a day off, but she made a mental note to take even more vitamin C, just in case.

While doing her pre-show ritual of checking on her props and costumes, Wendy couldn't help observing how different the atmosphere of the theatre was. Instead of the excited and frantic energy that usually radiated throughout the building, there was a sluggish exhaustion hanging over them. There was no more gentle mocking or running around; instead, people were barely speaking and were leaning against walls or sitting on any surface they could find. It seemed that some of the troupe were doing as little as possible in order to save up enough energy to make it through the show. Even Gerard and Carina were too tired to flirt.

Wendy's usual nervousness increased to an almost unsettling point. They'd done shows where a person or two were having an off night and the rest of the troupe had to compensate, but never had there been so many people at one time. There was an actual potential for everything to crash and burn, despite their best efforts.

Jim would be furious if they messed this up and displeased their patron. Although he seemed just as exhausted as everyone else, there was no limit to his energy when it came to being upset.

Wendy desperately hoped that they'd make it through the show unscathed.

The first act went well, all things considered. Francesca was on-point as always, although Wendy suspected that she could be two seconds from death and still give an amazing performance. Gerard was more forgetful than usual, but Francesca covered it well, having had many opportunities to deal with his lack of line-learning. There were a few flubs and errors throughout each of the sketches, and Carina seemed spacier than usual, sometimes staring off absently when she was supposed to be listening to another actor. Even Billy appeared to move slower during the scene changes.

However, it wasn't the train wreck that Wendy had been predicting. The audience sounded like they were enjoying themselves, even laughing when they caught someone messing up. Despite the low energy, everyone had been able to pull it together (for the most part), pretend that everything was fine, and get the job done.

When she thought about it, Wendy had to hold back a laugh. Wasn't that what actors did best? Pretend?

The second act had a rough start after intermission, with 'Mime the Musical,' which was a strange enough concept anyway, but at least it didn't require any set or props or dialogue. The pace picked up with 'Dating Sports,' where commentators provided a running commentary for two people training for upcoming dates, and continued to increase right up to the final skit. Thankfully, the show ended on a high note with 'The School of Hard Knocks,' a skit about a no-nonsense teacher whipping her students into shape by teaching them important life skills, like doing taxes and reading up on rental laws. Part of the reason for the success was that the teacher was played by Francesca, who was giving a perfect performance, walking a fine line between tough and knowledgeable.

Although the show ended with roaring applause from the audience, as soon as the curtains closed, it felt as if the entire stage exhaled wearily. Actors stopped smiling and let out sighs or yawns, and designers leaned against walls or collapsed into chairs, no longer able to stand. Instead of the mad rush to get everything put away before the party, there was a weary recognition that there was still more work to be done.

Wendy followed Stacey and Carina down to the dressing room, being careful not to show too much energy, lest they get annoyed at her for having some.

"We've earned this party," Stacey said, pulling off her costume. "This has been the week from hell and back again."

Carina nodded and yawned, leaning against the counter. "Next time I think I'll ask Jim to write me out of all the skits."

"Hopefully the next show will be a lot simpler," Wendy said as she changed. "If it isn't, the entire troupe might revolt against Jim."

"Now that sounds like fun," Stacey smirked.

They finished getting ready in silence, but Wendy noticed that Stacey was starting to get her second wind and her mood was improving. Carina, however, was still slow and lagging behind. Wendy wondered how many late nights she'd had with Gerard. Surely it wasn't worth the two of them being this tired and rundown.

The designers were still busy putting things away as the three women left the theatre. Wendy expected a few of them to make jokes or talk about the cast party, but nobody said anything. They all kept their heads down and did their jobs. Suppressing a shudder, Wendy tried not to think about how the theatre had changed so completely in only two weeks. Hopefully, now that the variety show was over, they'd all get a chance to rest and feel better. *Phantom* was going to be tough enough, and it'd be best for everyone if they had a chance to recuperate from the past week.

When they reached The Treehouse, the atmosphere was just as subdued, but at least they could all sit down with a drink in hand and didn't have to worry about performing. The conversation wasn't as animated as usual, and their voices barely rose above a level tone, but Wendy could see people perking up and genuine smiles on their faces.

Although Wendy felt fine, she was thankful for the quieter party. This week had been even more stressful than when she'd first joined the troupe, and she wasn't sure she'd make it through tomorrow's rehearsal if she partied too hard. As fun as their usual gatherings were, she was grateful for the chance to conserve energy.

As she glanced around at the tired, cheerful faces in the bar, Wendy hoped that the troupe would manage to find some of the life and energy that the past two weeks had sapped from them.

CHAPTER TWENTY-FOUR

Ari walked through the lower level slowly, keeping an out to see if there was anybody still down there. Normally they'd go to the cast party with the last few designers, but the show seemed to have worn everyone out, and they wanted to make sure nobody got left behind. It wouldn't be too surprising to find someone curled up, asleep, in one of the rooms.

It was incredible that the show had gone as well as it did. Ari had noticed that some strange virus seemed to be making its way through the troupe, lowering people's energy and creating a lack-luster effort backstage. Either that or people were getting tired of Jim's crazy rehearsal schedule—which was a very plausible excuse. Jim was getting dangerously close to the edge with this project, putting so much pressure on everyone to make *Phantom* the best thing the theatre had ever done, while refusing to cut back on the variety show. They made a mental note to keep a close eye on everyone over the next week to make sure Jim didn't push the cast or crew any harder.

As Ari walked through the hallway, they heard the knocking of the pipes and made a second mental note to remind Jim to get someone in to look at the furnace. Although they were sure it was nothing, they didn't want to risk this being part of a bigger problem and causing more trouble in the future.

Making their way towards the stairs, Ari heard the knocking increase as they passed by the basement door. Shaking their head, they started to go up the stairs, but then they heard a sound, almost like someone groaning.

Rolling their eyes, Ari pushed open the door to the basement and stuck their head through.

"If you're mucking about down there, get your act together and go home! I don't have time for this nonsense!"

The noise instantly stopped and the theatre fell deathly silent. Ari headed up to the next floor, frowning and shaking their head.

CHAPTER TWENTY-FIVE

Tapping her pencil absent-mindedly on the side of her desk, Betty tried to concentrate on her work, but her mind kept going back to the strange mood within the theatre. Normally when she passed people in the hallway they'd smile and say "hello," but these days they were barely able to raise their head and grunt some kind of greeting. Everyone seemed to be lost in their own world, occupied by thoughts of their work, with no room for anything else. She wished that there was a way for everyone to take a break for a few days, so that they could get some rest and catch up, but there wasn't enough time.

She was also feeling stressed by the amount of work before them, but for the first time in a long time she had a notion that other people were worse off than her. It wasn't a good feeling.

It didn't help that her thoughts were also preoccupied by her worries about Galia. The chandelier effect had consumed her sister's every waking thought. Even with help from Billy and her, Galia wasn't yet satisfied with the effect and so wasn't able to let it go. She'd finished all the other special effects, so her brain was entirely focused on this one. As the days passed, Galia stayed at the theatre later and later, and whenever she was at the apartment, she walked around like a zombie—her mind totally consumed by thoughts of falling chandeliers.

Betty tried to tell herself that the effect would soon be complete, and her sister would go back to normal, but those thoughts provided little comfort. It would be impossible for any of them to relax until the show's run was over.

Tugging at her hair, she tried once more to focus on her work. She still had to finish staining the barrels of gunpowder for the scene in the Phantom's lair, and there were plenty more letters for her to write, but the multiple worries bobbing around in her head refused to let her concentrate.

Finally she realized that if she didn't get some actual work done, it would stress her out more and she might end up a walking zombie like everyone else. Taking in a deep breath, she put her head down and made a list of four things she needed to accomplish today. Once the list was real and tangible, she made a promise to her worries that she'd get back to them soon and got to work.

When she finished two hours later, she didn't feel any better. There should have been some relief at completing her list, but something was bothering her, poking at the insides of her brain. Tapping her pencil against the desk again, she wondered if it was her worries about her sister or everyone else in the troupe, or if it was something deeper.

The answer hit her like a ton of bricks. It was Wendy. It was keeping their relationship secret from her sister. Being constantly on edge and worrying that she might let something slip or say the wrong thing was exhausting; so was worrying that her sister might say something to make her feel even worse. That anxiety had been slowly gnawing away at her, ripping her up inside, and had been doing so for a long time.

A part of her brain told her that she was overreacting and that all this worry and build-up was for nothing. Surely her sister wouldn't care who she dated. There were plenty of people in the theatre who dated all kinds of people, so if Galia didn't mind that, surely she wouldn't mind her sister dating someone of the same sex. Right?

But then her mind flashed back to her parents and all the terrible things they'd said about anyone who didn't fit into the "norm." What if all their poisonous rhetoric had settled into Galia's subconscious? What if what was okay for other people wasn't okay for her family?

Unfortunately, there was only one way to find out.

Taking in a deep breath, Betty rose to her feet, sending her chair scraping back along the floor. That was it—she was going to do it now and get it over with, and she'd deal with the fallout later. (She really hoped that there wouldn't be any fallout.)

Marching into the hall, she headed to the special effects room, finding Galia leaning against her drafting table, her chin resting in one hand, and her eyes half-closed.

"Galia?" Betty took a tentative step into the room, all her determination getting pushed aside as concern for her sister rose to the surface. "Are you okay?"

Galia looked up, and Betty could see the dark bags under her eyes. "Just tired. Still trying to figure out a way to make that chandelier fall look good."

"I thought it looked good yesterday when you tested it."

Galia rolled her eyes. "It looked *okay* yesterday, if you think a boring chandelier fall is good enough."

"I don't think there's such a thing," Betty countered.

Galia sighed and leaned back in her chair. "It's still too slow. I want the audience to feel like it's going to fall on their heads and that they're going to be smashed under it. I know I can do it. I just need to figure it out..."

Betty walked over to her, standing near the desk. "Sis, I know you want to do a great job, but I don't want you killing yourself over this. Maybe you should go home and sleep. In fact, when was the last time you had a full night's rest?"

Galia shrugged. "When have any of us slept a full night ever?"

"You know, that's probably something we should change," Betty said hesitantly. "If we're not careful, the whole troupe's going to pass out from exhaustion."

"It's nothing we haven't done before," Galia replied, waving off her concerns with her hand. "We'll rest when we're dead."

Betty frowned but didn't respond. She'd never liked that phrase.

"So, what do you need my help with?" Galia asked.

"What?"

"I'm assuming you're in here because you need my help. Or are you checking up on me?"

Betty looked down at her feet. She tried to bring back the determination that had brought her into the room, but she could only muster up fifty percent of it. It would have to be enough. "I..." she paused and looked up at her sister. "I want to talk to you about my relationship."

Galia sighed. "When are you moving out?"

"What?" She was so taken aback by the comment that she almost physically took a step backwards. "No, I'm not moving out."

"But you're spending more time away from home." Galia suddenly sat up straighter. "Oh, am I finally going to meet your mystery man?"

Betty felt her entire body crumple. Her face fell and she was filled with the urge to run from the room and never come back.

"What's wrong?" Galia said, slowly standing up from her chair. "Did I say something wrong?"

Betty sighed, frustration filling her body and propelling her forward. "You know what? Yeah, you did. And you keep doing it, and that's the problem."

Galia stared at her as concern and confusion crossed her face, but Betty didn't allow herself to stop.

"You keep saying things like 'him' and 'man,' and I keep getting crushed under the weight of those expectations. You have such a clear idea of things in your head, and I can't live up to them. I wanted to tell you ages ago, but I couldn't stop myself from drowning in all the terrible things that might happen if I did, and I didn't want to risk our relationship if I didn't have to. I didn't want to lose you, like we lost mom and dad." Betty saw Galia's expression fall as she started to put the pieces together.

"Betty, I would never toss you out because of who you love..." Galia put her hands to her head. "Was I really that narrow-minded? Oh my god, I can be such an idiot some-times. I'm so sorry I did that to you."

"So, you really wouldn't care if I wasn't dating a guy?" Betty asked, her voice quiet and small.

Galia went over and wrapped her up in a big hug. "Sis, I don't care who you're dating, as long as they treat you right and you're happy."

Betty wrapped her arms around her sister and hugged her tightly. "Thanks."

When they broke apart, Betty felt a giant wave of relief wash over her. She'd been so nervous for so long, and it had all been for nothing.

"So," Galia said, smiling, "who is the person you're dating?"

"It's... Wendy."

Galia paused. "So, you're dating an actor?"

Betty burst out laughing. "Shut up."

"I'm just saying... they're notoriously crazy."

"Well, I've had lots of practice from living with you."

"Touché."

The two of them looked at each other and large smiles broke out on their faces.

Betty took in a deep breath. It felt as if the air was clearer and easier to breath. "Now that that's over with, I want you to promise me that you'll take care of yourself. Get some sleep tonight."

"I'll try, sis," Galia said, sitting back at her table. "Maybe if I add another safety line, Ari will let me drop it faster..."

Betty started to leave, but then she turned back. "Oh, do you know if there's any extra spray paint in the basement?

Jim suddenly wants the lantern spray-painted silver, and I used my last can on the knives, so I need more."

"The basement?" Galia immediately stood up from the table, almost sending her chair to the floor. "No, there's nothing down there. Don't bother looking."

"Are you okay?" Betty said carefully, taken aback by Galia's violent reaction.

"Yeah. Just don't go down there, okay? Promise?"

"Why not?"

Galia paused. "I've got a feeling. It's hard to explain. It's like a skin-crawling, terrible, horrible feeling. Just avoid the basement, okay? Please."

Betty didn't understand why her sister sounded so wary. If she didn't know any better, she'd say that Galia sounded scared. "All right, I won't go down there. I mean, the furnace and the knocking are creepy enough, right? I'm more than happy to stay away."

Galia nodded, but it was an absent-minded movement. She pulled the chair back and sat down, her energy suddenly low and subdued. "Yeah..."

"Galia?" Betty said cautiously.

It was like a switch flipped and instantly her sister was back to her old, tired self. "Thanks for finishing the chandelier so quickly. And so far, the pieces are all staying on, so good work. I'm going to do some more thinking, but I'll let you know when we're ready to do another test."

The change was so sudden that Betty wondered if she'd been mistaken about before, but the unease of her sister's words about the basement still resonated in her mind. Deciding not to bring it back up, she nodded. "Thanks. I can't wait to see what you come up with."

Betty turned to leave again.

"Oh, one last thing."

"Yeah?" Betty turned around, curious about what her sister might say. Was it another strange warning?

"I'm genuinely happy for you and Wendy." She smirked. "Even if she is an *actor*."

Unable to hold back her grin, Betty nodded and left the room.

Before Wendy had a chance to call out that the door was open, Betty burst into the apartment. The sudden arrival startled Wendy, and she instinctively backed up against the kitchen counter, wondering what had gone wrong. When she saw the look of elation on Betty's face, however, she quickly realized that everything was okay.

"I did it!" Betty said, raising her hands in triumph. She bounded over to Wendy, her eyes bright and sparkling with joy. "I told Galia!"

Wendy's mouth dropped open in surprise. She could tell by Betty's reaction that the conversation had gone well and grinned widely. "Congratulations!" she said, sweeping Betty up in a big hug.

Betty's lips found hers, and when they kissed it felt just as magical as the first time.

Wendy was overjoyed that they no longer had to keep their affection hidden. They could hold hands at the theatre and walk down the street together. She could even visit Betty in the props room more often.

"I'm so proud of you!" Wendy said. "And I'm relieved she took it well."

Betty smirked. "Well, she is a little disappointed that I'm dating an actor, but she'll get over it."

Wendy rolled her eyes, but the smile never disappeared from her face. "We should celebrate!"

Although they were both feeling invigorated by the good news, they decided to stay in and order food, and celebrate on their own. But instead of one of them picking up the food, this time they went together.

There was a chill in the winter air, but there was no snow on the ground. They held hands as they walked past the streetlights that illuminated the small cobblestone street, and Betty filled Wendy in on how her conversation with Galia had gone. Wendy was surprised that Betty had lost her temper, but she was glad that it had helped her get over her nerves. She was also relieved that Galia had been so accepting, because she knew how much it meant to Betty to have her sister on her side.

They picked up their food at Electric Lunch and then headed to Rainbow Bites to get something sweet for dessert. One of the many perks of living on this street was having a small bakery that stayed open late to satisfy any sweet cravings that might pop up.

Still holding hands, they smiled brightly as they walked along the cobblestone street, back to Wendy's apartment.

CHAPTER TWENTY-SIX

She was standing on the stage, all alone, with an empty audience in front of her. It was like the last time, with numerous unseen people watching her, but there was one big difference. Hanging above the invisible audience, glittering in the dim light, was a gigantic chandelier.

There was something beautiful, yet ominous about it. It was made of razor-sharp pieces of crystal, keen enough to slice the air in two. The audience it was perched over seemed oblivious of the danger above them.

A knock sounded behind her and she felt her heart jump in her chest.

"Stop!" she yelled at nobody in particular; her voice filling the empty room. "Go away! Leave us alone!"

Silence.

The eyes continued to watch.

Breathing heavily, she realized that she could make out faint shapes in a few of the seats. Transparent black smoke had somehow appeared and formed human-like shapes. It was still impossible to make out any features, but she could see that there were thirteen people watching her. Were they the spirits of everyone who'd died in the theatre?

The knocking started up again, but instead of coming from behind it was now coming from above. Her gaze moved up to the chandelier. The crystals began to glow an ominous red, reminding her of drops of blood. With each knock the entire structure shook, and the hundreds of crystals making up the chandelier rattled violently.

She knew what the chandelier was supposed to do. It was supposed to fall, to kill someone, just like the Phantom wanted. He had warned them that they needed to obey, and they hadn't. Now they were going to pay the price.

As the ominous chandelier continued to shake with each knock, pieces began to break off, falling into the audience like drops of blood spilling from a wound. None of the dark shapes seemed disturbed by it, and she could still feel their gaze on her, never wavering. They weren't afraid of the chandelier because they knew that it couldn't hurt them. They were made of smoke, not flesh and bone.

Her however...

Was that why they were here? To watch her be crushed by the chandelier? Did they want to see her die?

A loud noise shook the entire building, including the stage underneath her unmoving feet. The rigging holding the chandelier gave a loud creak and she could hear wires snapping. Her eyes widened as the chandelier dropped and began to swing towards her.

"Wendy! Wake up!"

Her eyes snapped open. She was in her bed, the room half-lit by the rising sun. "What...? Betty?"

Betty was leaning over her, concern filling her green eyes. "You were tossing and turning and seemed really scared. What was going on? Were you having a night-mare?"

Wendy tried to think back to the dream, grabbing onto as many details as she could before they disappeared.

"It was bad," she said, piecing together the fragments as she pulled herself into a sitting position. "I was at the theatre, on the stage, but nobody else was there. But there were people in the audience, except they weren't people, they were more like spirits..." She shook her head, wondering if Betty was able to make any sense of what she was saying. "There was a chandelier. The knocking started and it was loud enough to shake the whole building. The chandelier was shaking, and pieces were raining down on the audience, but then it fell and started swinging right for me."

Betty let out a breath. "That sounds terrifying."

Wendy nodded and sighed. "I think I'm just nervous about the show."

"You shouldn't be. You're doing great."

She wanted to smile, but those words filled her with dread. "But how else am I supposed to explain these dreams? I keep hearing that I'm doing great and I feel good about what I'm doing, but these nightmares won't go away." Fear suddenly overwhelmed her and an image of the basement door glowing red flashed in her mind. "I know it sounds weird, Betty, but I feel like there's a monster in the basement. There's something at the theatre that isn't right. Everyone's walking around like zombies, and I don't think it's because Jim's pushed us too far. Something's really wrong."

When she looked over at Betty, she noticed a conflict-ed expression on her face.

"I don't know what to say," Betty said carefully. "I mean, I don't believe in ghosts, but I agree that everyone seems more rundown than usual. If it's the flu, then it's the weirdest strain I've ever seen." She paused, suddenly remembering something from yesterday. "There was something Galia said, after I talked to her. I mentioned going down in the basement and she told me not to. She didn't have a good reason for it, but she seemed scared."

Wendy's eyes widened at this new information. Did Galia also suspect that there was an evil spirit in the basement?

"She couldn't explain it, and I don't know what to think about it," Betty continued. "There's got to be a logical explanation for all of this, but I don't know what it is, or why the basement creeps out so many people when we've been around it for years."

"I'd love for there to be a logical explanation," Wendy said, sighing. It wasn't a lie. She wanted nothing more than to make things go back to the way they were, and if all this ghost talk turned out to be nothing, then she'd be relieved. However, the evidence seemed to be lining up in favour of something that couldn't be easily explained. "...But I think we should both avoid the basement either way."

Although Betty didn't think that there was anything down there to be afraid of—other than a temperamental furnace that might explode—she nodded. When the two people she cared about most told her to avoid a place, she had no choice but to do so.

CHAPTER TWENTY-SEVEN

Their show opened in two days and Wendy wasn't sure if they were going to make it. They'd run through the entire show twice yesterday, but there was a lot that needed to be fixed. Gerard still didn't know his lines, Carina and Stacey were low energy and late for entrances, Billy had so many cues that he missed half of them, and most of the costumes still needed work. Jim's note sessions after each run-through went on for so long that even he seemed tired of hearing his own voice.

Wendy had been optimistic about Monday's rehearsal, seeing as how the day before was their day off and everyone would have a chance to sleep in and get some rest, but there was so much to be done that she doubted anyone rested. Even she had spent half of the day going over her script at home.

Although they'd run through the show on stage instead of in the rehearsal hall, they didn't run most of the effects, including the chandelier drop, for which Wendy was thankful. Even though Francesca would be in a much more precarious position than her when the drop happened, her nightmare had made her particularly nervous about that effect.

Betty, Galia, Billy, Ari, and Jim had come in early that morning to run it a few times, so that it'd be ready for the afternoon's cue-to-cue. While Wendy knew that Ari wouldn't let any potentially dangerous effects happen, she couldn't help feeling on edge every time she looked up at the massive chandelier hanging above them.

Normally Wendy found cue-to-cues extremely long and boring. They involved running through the show, but only going from one cue to the next, and although most of the dialogue was skipped, it often took twice as long as a run-through. Even though the creative team worked hard beforehand to get the cues ready, there was always a risk that Jim wouldn't like the timing or that something would need adjusting. Since the actors were needed to perform their entrances and exits and give out cue lines, they usually spent a lot of time standing or sitting around, waiting for their next cue.

This show was so elaborate that Wendy had suspected they'd be here for twenty-four hours in order to run through all the light, sound, and effects cues, but it was moving along at a good pace. It likely had to do with how tired Jim looked. Whenever he was too exhausted to nitpick, Ari would quickly move everyone on to the next cue.

When she wasn't needed on stage, Wendy managed to keep busy by watching everyone else, looking for signs of illness or something more sinister. Some people seemed tired but fine, but most were looking even worse than before. Whenever they weren't needed, they usually sat around, not doing anything, acting like listless zombies.

Was it her imagination or did their skin look grey?

She wondered if they'd opened some kind of Pandora's Box when they decided to do this play, releasing a curse over the theatre and everyone inside.

Betty nervously watched as Ari gave the cue for the chandelier. They'd run through the drop three times earlier and everything had worked great, but this was their first time running it in sequence. Ari had suggested that they run the cue first with nobody on stage, to give the actors a chance to get used to it, and then reset and run it a second time with the actors. There was a groaning from a few people about having to do such an elaborate cue twice, but that wasn't enough to stop it from happening.

Even though Betty was already looking at the ceiling and knew exactly what was going to happen, the popping and sparking of the small pyro charges around the edge of the chandelier startled her. After the charges finished, the chandelier dropped down and started to swing towards the stage in a wide arc. The theatre plummeted into darkness as the lights went out, and when they came back on a few seconds later, the curtains were closed and the chandelier was nowhere to be seen.

There was a round of applause from everyone sitting in the auditorium. Even though Betty knew that Galia had pushed herself to the point of exhaustion to get this effect perfected, it didn't stop her from jumping up and pumping a fist in the air in triumph.

Breathing a sigh of relief, Betty slid down in her chair and allowed herself to relax a bit more. It was a good thing she'd taken extra care to attach the fake crystal pieces on the chandelier, as not a single one of them had fallen off all day.

Now they just had to try it with the actors on stage.

The curtains opened and Galia moved on stage to help monitor the chandelier's rise, while Billy and Ari headed to the lighting grid to pull it back up to the ceiling. Betty was glad that she was able to witness this effect from off-stage. If she'd been an actor and had to stand there, watching that swinging towards her, she'd freak out.

Suddenly she was reminded of Wendy's dream on Sunday morning, about being on stage and watching the chandelier coming straight for her. Her mind wandered back to that conversation, and how sure Wendy had seemed that something wasn't right at the theatre. Betty had been so certain that there was a reasonable explanation behind it all, but over the past few days she'd found her confidence wavering.

She'd seen illnesses pass through the building before, and the cast and creative had been overworked many, many times—especially when she'd first been hired—but this was a completely new occurrence. Watching people closely, she could see that it was almost like they were having their energy sucked out of them. It had bothered her so much that she'd gone online to see if there were reports of a strange new flu that was affecting people in this way, but there was nothing. Nobody else on Jacobi Street seemed to be affected by it. It was like it was limited to their building.

Every rational explanation she came up with didn't fit. She'd even asked Ari about the possibility of there being mold in the building, but Ari said that it had been inspected four months ago and passed. But what else could it be? Even if ghosts were real, they couldn't affect people like this. Or could they?

When the cue-to-cue finally finished, Jim declared that there was enough time to do a full run of the show before calling it a night. Although the day had been a long and tedious one, he said that going through the show would help further cement everything in their minds.

It wasn't a smooth run by any means. Cues were missed, lines were forgotten, and props were mislaid, but they managed to get through it all without any serious incidents. By the end even Jim was too tired to give notes. He merely looked at everyone and told them, "You know what you did wrong," and called it a night.

They all trudged to their various workshops and dressing rooms, too tired to say anything. Wendy's thoughts were swirling around in her head as she made her way to the private dressing room backstage that she'd been given because she was a lead role. Francesca had her usual room, while the other two had been given to Vance and Gerard. She noticed that Francesca seemed fine, other than being annoyed at the imperfect run, and so did Vance, but Gerard was flat-out exhausted. In Wendy's mind there were two groups of people: those who were tired but healthy, and those who seemed to be having their energy sucked out by some unseen ghost. She didn't like how long the latter list was.

After changing out of her costume, she sat down at

the counter, and tried to make sense of what was going on at the theatre. Could it be a curse? Or was it a vengeful ghost, hiding in the basement, draining everyone else's energy to make itself stronger? It sounded impossible and ridiculous, but also made more sense than anything else she could come up with. If it were an illness, then surely there'd be some kind of medicine that would help them feel better. There was no way that so many people would feel so terrible and not do anything to help themselves.

But how was a person supposed to fight against a ghost?

Putting her head in her hands, she wondered how things had gone so wrong. This was supposed to be her dream role, but how could she enjoy it when so many people were feeling terrible? How was she supposed to help when she had no idea what was going on?

There was a knocking on her door that startled her, but she quickly realized that it was a person knocking and not the terrible sound from the basement.

"Come in," she called out, quickly pulling herself together.

Betty poked her head in through the door. When she noticed that Wendy was alone, she slipped into the room, closing the door behind her.

"I think you're right," Betty said, her voice full of uncertainty, as if unable to believe what she was saying. "Something's wrong here. I've seen people sick and tired and overworked, but this is completely different, and I don't know what it is, but it's unnatural."

Normally Wendy liked being right, but this time she felt no satisfaction. "I don't know what it is either, but I think it might be a spirit. Something in this building is draining the life from certain people, and I don't know why it's attacking them and not everyone, but maybe it only has a limited reach?"

"So, what do we do?" Betty walked into the room and leaned against the counter. "There has to be something we can do to fix it. Right? We need to figure out what's going on and make it stop, and then everything will go back to normal."

Wendy was about to say that she had no idea what to do, but then the image of the basement door popped in her mind. "I think we need to go to the basement," she said cautiously. "I think there's something down there that's causing all of this."

Normally Betty wouldn't be scared to go anywhere in the building, but Galia's warnings about the basement were still fresh in her mind. Her certainty that supernatural creatures did not exist had been shaken, and she was actually feeling afraid.

Pulling herself together, she summoned up all her courage. If Wendy could suggest such a thing when she was obviously scared, then she could handle it. After all, she'd promised Wendy that if she needed her, she'd be there to hold her hand.

"Should we go down now?" Betty asked.

At the suggestion Wendy felt her heart leap in her throat and her pulse quicken. She was definitely not prepared to face the basement right now. "No, this day's been too long and insane. Let's do it tomorrow night, after midnight, when everyone's gone. That'll give us time to prepare."

Betty nodded. "Tomorrow, then. What should we take with us? Crosses and holy water?"

She shrugged. "Salt, lighter fluid, and matches? Your guess is as good as mine."

"I'll do some research." Betty paused. "What do you think we'll find?"

A thousand terrible things raced through Wendy's mind, but she didn't want to say any of them. Instead, she decided to be honest: "I don't know."

CHAPTER TWENTY-EIGHT

On the night of the dress rehearsal, the whole troupe gathered in the audience to listen to Jim's motivational speech. He gave the same speech every time, no matter what they were doing—whether it be a play or a sketch show—so most of them knew it by heart. But there was something about the way Jim was speaking this time that wasn't the same. He sounded tired, just like everyone else looked. Instead of the excitement of being one day away from opening night, it felt as if he was trying to ward off an ill omen.

Once the speech was over, Wendy hurried to get into her first costume. She tried to tell herself that it was only a rehearsal and that she was prepared for almost everything. And even if things went wrong, wasn't there a saying in the theatre: "bad dress rehearsal, good opening night"? She quickly changed into her costume and put on her make-up. When Ari gave the places call over the speaker, Wendy felt her breath catch in her throat. She took a few deep, calming breaths and left her dressing room.

As nervous as she was beforehand, it didn't affect her performance, and whenever she was on stage she felt

confident and prepared. However, the minute her character left a scene, everything seemed off. The wings looked
darker than usual, everyone's attitude was quiet, and the
overall mood was more intense. Normally she'd spend
most of her free time watching from the wings, but today
she stayed in her dressing room until it was close to her
next cue, away from everyone else and their strange behaviour.

She was thankful when the show ended. As amazing
as it was to be playing this part, she wanted to shake off
the unsettled feeling that had increased during the dress
rehearsal. She felt that she'd done well, but other actors
had forgotten lines and missed cues, and even though everyone had tried to compensate for it, she knew that it had
been a terrible performance. If Betty and she weren't able
to figure out what was causing this strange behaviour,
then this show was doomed.

She'd just finished changing into her street clothes
when there was a knock on her dressing room door. She
opened it to see Vance standing on the other side.

"Yes?" she asked, startled by his appearance. They'd
gotten along well enough during rehearsals, but he'd never made much of an effort to talk to her before or after.

"I know I'm new to this," he said, looking around to
make sure that nobody was listening, "but are we actually
ready to open this show or is it going to get cancelled?"

She opened her mouth to say something flippant, but
then thought better of it. She also thought better of telling
him her suspicions.

"No," she shook her head. "This is some kind of weird
flu or something. I think everyone's saving their energy

for tomorrow."

"I hope so," he said, a concerned look on his face. "My partner's got a ticket for tomorrow, and I'd hate for it to not happen."

"It was a pretty bad run," Wendy admitted, "but I've seen worse when it comes to our variety shows, and we always manage to pull it together by showtime."

He seemed slightly reassured. "That's good to hear. I've been having fun doing this, and I'd hate for all our hard work not to pay off."

"You've been having fun?" Wendy said before quickly slapping a hand over her mouth. She couldn't believe she'd said such a rude statement out loud. "I'm sorry! I didn't mean to say that! It's just that in rehearsals you don't... I mean, it's not obvious... Oh god..." She wanted to crawl under the counter and die.

To her complete surprise, Vance laughed. "I get it, okay? I haven't been the most outgoing person." He gave a half-shrug. "You're all so familiar with each other and sure about what you're doing, and sometimes it feels like I'm on the outside looking in."

Taking a moment, Wendy thought about how it must have been for Vance to come into this crazy troupe. She'd had an easier time, but it was mostly because Stacey and Carina had decided she wasn't much of a threat and added her to their group, and because Francesca helped her out. Gerard and Sam were too self-centred to help anyone, and she'd been so preoccupied with her own role that she hadn't thought to check in on him.

"Do you have a moment?" she asked. "Because if you're interested, I can tell you a bunch of gossip about everyone in this building. It'll be like you've known them forever."

He looked at his watch and nodded, a large smile crossing his face. "I've got some time."

As Wendy motioned for him to enter her dressing room, she felt a grin cross her own face. First, she was going to make Vance feel like more of the team, and then later tonight she and Betty were going to find that evil spirit and kick its ass into the next century.

CHAPTER TWENTY-NINE

The bright glow of the ghost light's single bulb was almost blinding in the darkness, but its reach wasn't far enough to illuminate the entire auditorium. Instead, it lent a faint glow to any objects farther than four feet away, outlining the shape but not providing any detail.

The theatre was dark and silent as Betty and Wendy made their way through the auditorium, using Betty's keys to let them in. They'd checked that all the lights in Jim's apartment had been out before entering the building, not wanting him to accidentally wander down and find them. If someone dared question what they were doing, Wendy had a feeling that she'd lose all nerve and run away, and she wanted to get this over and done with. Whatever *this* was.

Wendy was carrying a purse that contained multiple lighters, candles, filtered water, a steak knife, and some salt. Meanwhile, Betty had decided to bring a large pipe wrench that was almost as long as her arm. Hopefully it would be enough.

As they walked, Wendy thought she could see people sitting in the audience out of the corner of her eye, but when she turned to look at them, the seats were empty. Outlined by the glow of the ghost light, Wendy wasn't sure if her feeling of being watched by an invisible audience was real or something that she was creating all on her own.

The two of them made their way through the backstage and down to the lower level, exchanging an uneasy look as they stopped in front of their destination. The door to the basement looked more innocent than it had in months. The colour had gone back to a faded dark red and looked nothing like blood. There was no eerie glowing coming from behind, and even the chipped paint looked more like normal flaking and not something being forcibly peeled back.

"You okay?" Betty asked, her voice low and soft even though they were the only people in the building.

Wendy nodded. "I hate it, but I'm going to do it anyway." She reached out for the door, but before she could put her hand on the doorknob, it creaked open. She looked back at Betty, whose eyes had gone wide.

"It's just the air, it's just the air, it's just the air..." Betty muttered to herself over and over, her breath coming quickly. She lifted the pipe wrench higher, holding it like a baseball bat.

Taking in a shaky breath, Wendy gripped the flashlight tighter and stepped through the door. She'd half-expected the landing to crumble as soon as both of her feet were on it, but although it let out a low groan, it stayed up. Swallowing hard, she flicked on the light switch near the door. Instead of all the overhead lights turning on, only the ones in the middle of the room lit up, creating a path for her to follow to the back of the room. She didn't like it.

Every step she took, she expected something terrible to happen, like for her foot to break through the step and get stuck, or for something to grab at her legs through the stairs. The fact that nothing happened was almost worse. Other than the door opening on its own and the strange way the lights had turned on, there was nothing out of the ordinary. Was the basement trying to lull her into a false sense of security?

"Where to?" Betty asked once they'd both stepped off the stairs and onto the floor.

Wendy shone her flashlight to either side, illuminating the darkened areas. Around them were old backgrounds and set pieces. Although being down here gave her the creeps, there was nothing about this area that was particularly chilling, so she pressed forward, following the path of the overhead lights.

They moved at a slow pace, with Wendy shining her light over everything along the sides, making sure that nothing was going to jump out at them. Perhaps this was an elaborate joke orchestrated by Stacey and Carina, to make her think she was crazy as revenge for her getting the role of Christine. Maybe they'd involved the entire troupe, except for Betty, and now they were waiting in the shadows to jump out and laugh at how gullible she was. If that was the case, then she'd be relieved. Furious as hell, but still relieved.

Unfortunately, as they neared the furnace, Wendy realized that perhaps it wasn't a joke.

"What is that?" Betty whispered, drawing closer to her.

"I don't know." Wendy stepped forward and stared at the large red circle that was painted on the floor of the basement, tucked into the space between the furnace and the wall. There was a large triangle painted in the middle of the circle, with each point touching the edge of the circle but not going outside. Another circle had been drawn in the middle of the triangle, separating the three points, and inside each point were strange squiggly lines. Each squiggle was different, and she had no idea what any of them meant or what language they were supposed to be. In the centre of the circle was a low metal bowl filled with something that looked like ash or dust.

Betty frowned. "Is this a joke? Is someone trying to play a prank on us?"

Wendy wasn't sure what to say. She wanted to take a closer look, but she also wanted to run as far away from here as humanly possible. She'd seen enough movies to recognize that this had to be some kind of magic.

"Maybe it's a spell to sap people's energies..." Wendy said uncertainly.

A loud *bang* startled them, and they both jumped.

"What are you two doing here?"

They jumped again, but when they turned around, they saw Scott standing about six feet behind them. His eyes were narrowed and he looked like he hadn't slept in days. He was holding his clipboard loosely in his left hand.

"Oh, it's you, Scott," Betty said, lowering her pipe wrench. "What are you doing down here?"

"I heard you two talking last night. I wanted to see what you'd find."

Wendy frowned. Had he been listening outside her dressing room? It was creepy, but entirely in character for him. Maybe he also suspected that something weird was going on and was trying to figure it out.

"Look what we found," she said, pointing to the circle. "What do you think it is? It's got to have something to do with the crazy stuff happening around here, right?"

"Who do you think did it?" Betty asked as he glanced towards the circle. "I can't imagine anyone else doing something like this. Maybe it was Vance? We've known him the least amount of time."

Yesterday Wendy would have been on the same page, but now that she'd had time to get to know Vance, she was pretty sure he wasn't malicious enough to do something like this. But who else could it be?

Scott rolled his eyes. "Of course, you think it's Vance. He's all anyone thinks about these days."

Wendy and Betty exchanged a look. Was this really the time for jealousy?

"Vance didn't do this," Scott said angrily, absentmindedly tapping his clipboard against his leg.

"How do you know?" Betty asked.

"Because I'm the person who drew it!" Scott yelled, glaring daggers at them. "It's a summoning circle, you morons. And before you ask, I did it because I'm sick and tired of being treated like trash. You all look down on me as if I'm a useless bug. Jim refuses to let me assistant direct, the crew only acknowledges me when they need something, and the actors barely even know I exist. Unless I'm in the way, in which case you have no problem telling me what a waste of space I am. So I summoned this demon and trapped it down here, and once it's strong enough, it'll kill you all."

Wendy's mouth dropped open. She knew that Scott didn't like having to do menial tasks around the theatre and that some people gave him a hard time, but she had no idea that he was filled with so much hate. "What did you summon?"

Scott laughed. "As if I'm going to tell you."

Betty looked around, worry creasing her face. "Is it here?"

As if in answer to his question, a deep knocking sound reverberated throughout the basement.

"Fuck..." Betty muttered under her breath. "Fuck, fuck, fuck..."

"Get rid of it!" Wendy yelled. "Un-summon it or whatever."

Scott laughed bitterly. "Why would I do something like that?"

"Because it's hurting people!" Betty shouted as her eyes darted around the room.

"You've made your point," Wendy argued. "We get it, and we'll tell the others to stop giving you such a hard time. Now, get rid of that thing."

The sound reverberated again, louder this time. Scott rolled his eyes. "Whatever." He turned around to leave, but Betty raced forward and grabbed him by the shoulder, bringing him up short. His clipboard fell to the ground, clattering against the concrete.

"Take your hands off me," Scott ordered.

She tightened her grip. "Not until you get rid of this... thing."

Scott narrowed his eyes at her. "*Ad constringendum, ad ligandum eos pariter et solvendum: Et ad congregandum eos coram me.*"

The temperature in the room suddenly heated up. There was a scratching sound, like sharp objects being dragged along the side of the furnace. A low growl filled the room and Wendy had a bad feeling settle in her stomach.

"I'd ask you to take your hand off me again, but it's too late," Scott smirked.

Betty's hand dropped from Scott's shoulder as she noticed a large shadow rising behind him. The shadow seemed to be made of swirling air, black and dark purple, with two glowing red eyes.

"Oh, fuck fuck fuck fuck fuck..." Betty muttered, backing away from the shape.

Wendy' eyes widened in fear. She didn't know what the thing could do, but she wouldn't be surprised if its mouth was full of sharp, deadly teeth.

"HUNGRY," the creature said, its voice low and dark as death.

"Then get eating," Scott ordered, retrieving his clipboard. "Eat these two, and then I'll see about getting the rest of them down here."

"HUNGRY."

Scott rolled his eyes and started walking towards the staircase.

The beast looked down at Betty, its red eyes glowing menacingly. "HUNGRY."

Panic rose inside of Wendy. She didn't know what to do but knew that she had to do something. If she didn't, then she and Betty would never make it out of here alive. Turning back to the summoning circle, she made a split-second decision and kicked over the bowl, spreading ash all over the floor. When that didn't cause the beast to disappear, she drew the steak knife from her bag and started scratching at the paint on the circle. First, she'd un-summon this stupid demon, and then she'd deal with Scott.

The growling of the beast increased. Betty backed up almost to the wall, holding the pipe wrench in front of her, but the beast hadn't yet moved. It looked down at what Wendy was doing and then back at Scott.

Wendy scraped harder, desperately trying to scratch a line all the way through the paint and effectively breaking the circle. As soon as she did so, she was knocked off her feet by an invisible burst of energy.

"FREE."

Wendy stood up and scrambled over to Betty. Betty was still holding the wrench, but the beast was no longer looking at her. It had turned to Scott, who'd frozen in place, two feet away from the stairs.

"FREE."

Scott turned around and started whimpering as the beast approached. "No! You can't hurt me! I'm the one who summoned you!"

"TRAPPED."

Frantic noises escaped Scott's mouth. "No! Don't! Please! I'll get everyone down here faster! I'll send you back after you eat them all! I promise! Please!"

The beast drew closer. "HUNGRY."

Wendy watched in horror as the beast descended upon Scott. The screams he made would haunt her for a long time, but she didn't want to say or do anything that would put herself in the way of the beast.

When the screams stopped, she hoped that the beast would disappear, but instead it turned around, its glowing eyes watching her and Betty. The black and purple swirling air that made up its body were joined by swirls as red as blood. Wendy's breath came faster as she prepared herself for what was coming, but then the demon suddenly disappeared.

The basement went silent. There was no knocking, no screaming. Only quiet.

After what felt like an hour, Betty broke the silence.

"We should go."

Betty's words seemed to break the hold that was upon her and Wendy found herself able to move again. She took Betty's hand and they headed towards the stairs, ignoring the dark stain on the floor that was all that remained of Scott.

CHAPTER THIRTY

"Wendy?"

Wendy slowly opened her eyes. She felt groggy, as if she'd drank too much last night and was in that strange middle-ground that existed between drunk and hungover. When her eyes finally came into focus, she saw that she was lying in her bed, Betty sitting beside her, sleep still in the corners of her eyes, her red hair sticking out to one side.

"Did that happen last night? Was that real or a dream?" she asked.

Wendy tried to clear the fog from her mind as she pulled herself up into a sitting position. "Was your dream about us going in the basement, finding a demon, and watching it murder Scott?"

A grim look was on Betty's face as she nodded. "Dammit." A pained look crossed her face. "So, demons are real, and so is witchcraft, and our friends were having their life-force drained by a demon that Scott was keeping in the basement because he resented us all. How am I expected to do anything after all of that?"

Wendy reached out and took Betty's hand in hers. Last

night was weird and terrifying, but she'd grown up believing in spirits, so while the appearance of a demon was surprising, it wasn't out of the realm of possibility. Betty, who hadn't believed in the supernatural until a few days ago, had to come to terms with the fact that she'd watched a demon appear out of thin air and kill a person in front of her very eyes.

"Betty, I don't know what to say other than what happened last night was fucked up."

"It was *so* fucked up," Betty said.

"I don't know if we should try to tell the others what happened or if they'll think we're totally nuts. But hopefully that *thing* is gone, and we can all go back to normal."

Betty's eyes widened. "Do you think it's released everyone?"

Wendy was hit with two possibilities—one: that after the demon killed Scott, it went for everyone else; and two: that when the demon disappeared, its hold on everyone disappeared with it and they were all free. She hoped and prayed it was the latter. They'd find out soon enough, anyways, once they went to the theatre.

She suddenly realized that tonight was the opening night for *Phantom*, and the dread from last night was pushed aside by nerves. Looking over at her clock, her mouth dropped open as she realized that it was almost five in the afternoon. They'd slept for over twelve hours.

"The show's in three hours!" Wendy said, jumping up from the bed. "But is it even going to go on? What if everyone's still a mess?"

Seeing Wendy start to lose her mind, Betty found herself gaining back some control. Pushing aside thoughts of demons and death, she focused on the show—something she understood and had a modicum of control over.

"I think we should go to the theatre early," Betty said. "I mean, most of us designers usually go early. I think I'm actually late, to be honest. But we should get ready and go see how everyone is."

Wendy took a few deep breaths. "Yeah, you're right. We should get ready and go. And hopefully everything will be all right and everyone will be back to normal."

The two of them exchanged a look that was meant to be hopeful, but a note of uncertainty hung in the air.

As they walked backstage, the theatre was once again a flurry of activity, with crew and cast moving about, searching for props or costumes. Wendy's eyes widened as she saw Billy humming to himself and smiling as he checked on the ropes that pulled the backdrops up and down. There were still bags under his eyes, but he seemed to be in the best health of his life. Paloma also seemed to be feeling better, muttering to herself as she quickly went through the costume rack in the wings, checking that everything was still in order.

Wendy couldn't help staring. It was almost as if the past few weeks hadn't happened. A smile crossed her face. She looked over at Betty, who looked astonished.

"We did it..." Betty said softly, a smile slowly crossing her face. "Everything's back to normal."

Everything about the show was perfect, even with

Scott being a no-show. The first act went so smoothly that for a moment Wendy wondered if this was what it was like to be on Broadway or London's West End. Set pieces that might have been late coming in were perfectly timed, props that might have been moved accidentally were in their proper places, and lines that could have been dropped were said perfectly.

Now that the demon was gone, everything felt like a wonderful dream.

As they started the second half, Wendy threw herself into the performance. The masquerade scene was almost hypnotic. There seemed to be more people on stage than ever before, dancing and twirling. There was an intensity to the rooftop scene that she'd never felt before, and she heard audible gasps when the Phantom revealed himself at the end.

Wendy had never felt so alive. With the lights shining in her eyes, it was difficult to see the audience, but they made noises at the appropriate times, gasping and laughing whenever something astonishing or funny happened. One of them even shrieked when Christine ripped off the Phantom's mask, revealing the burned and scarred flesh that Galia had created from latex.

They finally reached the last scene of the play, after Christine and Raoul escaped the Phantom's torture chamber, running away as he screamed in agony. The stage was bare, but Jim had added a fake snowfall to provide atmosphere. Wendy saw Betty out of the corner of her eye, watching from the wings, before turning to Vance and saying her lines.

Finally, they kissed, and the play was over. The audience applauded loudly, cheering and jumping to their feet as the curtain came down. The designers and actors made their way onto the stage, ready for their bows. Even Jim joined them.

The curtain went up and Wendy stood near the centre of the stage, holding onto Vance and Gerard's hands as the group took a bow. But as they rose, her eyes caught something in the darkness, behind the audience. A cold, icy hand gripped her heart as the line of actors bowed again, taking her down with them. When they rose, Wendy looked back at the same area, noticing how one spot of darkness had taken on a purple and red hue, and how it almost seemed to be moving... swirling...

She glanced over at Betty and when their eyes met, she noticed that Betty also sensed something wasn't right.

Suddenly a number of stage lights went out, startling everyone. Wendy turned back to the dark, swirling purple smoke at the back of the room, but without so many lights focused on the stage, she was now able to see the audience better. She'd peeked out through the curtains before the show and noticed that the audience was almost three-quarters full, but now it seemed to be even fuller.

Some of the patrons looked strange, clad in odd outfits. There was someone dressed in full knight's regalia, another who looked like a nurse, another in an outfit from the 20s, and another in a powdered wig. It wasn't strange for people to dress up for shows, but these costumes didn't have anything to do with this show. Why were people wearing them?

Then she noticed that their former scenic painter was in the audience, along with the other people who had gone missing in the past month—Obi, the street artist; Mr. Cooper, the owner of Cooper's General Market; and Chelsea, the former owner of the Menagerie. What were they doing here? Had they all come back?

The swirling in the back of the theatre intensified, and Wendy's heart nearly stopped as the shape formed into that of the beast; two glowing red eyes appearing in the smoke. Wendy's eyes swept over the crowd, who seemed oblivious to the monster behind them. Suddenly scratches appeared on the thirteen strange audience members, lines of dark red drawn upon their skin, blood running down their arms and faces.

"FREE."

Wendy's breath caught in her throat. Half of the room looked around, confused at the strange noise, while the other half simply stared straight ahead.

"FREEDOM." The beast's deep voice boomed throughout the theatre.

The costumed strangers and the missing people suddenly disappeared. Wendy felt Gerard let go of her hand, and when she turned to look at him, he was lying on the floor. Her breath caught in her throat as other people fell with him—Stacey, Carina, Billy, Paloma, Jim, and Galia.

"What's happening?" Betty cried out, falling to her knees beside her sister.

Wendy couldn't answer. Turning back to the beast in the shadows, she knew the truth. When she'd broken the summoning circle, the beast hadn't been banished. Instead, it had been freed. Without Scott holding it back, it was able to devour anyone it wanted. And it had.

The beast let out a growl and disappeared from the back of the theatre, leaving the room in utter pandemonium. Wendy stared at the darkness, unable to move, as tears filled her eyes.

EPILOGUE

The faint chords drifted down the alley and out into the night air. At the back of the alley running between The Rashomon Gallery and The Hidden Forest Market, were two people. They were sitting on the stairs of the fire escape, barely illuminated by the dim light above the emergency exit door at the top of the staircase.

"Play the one about the underground tunnel to China," the young woman, Maireni, said, taking a long drag from the joint in her hand. Her eyes were glassy and the smile never left her face. Her hair was a light blue-green and she was dressed in multiple layers of clothing, with tops, sweaters, skirts, and scarves in bright colours. Crystals hung from her neck and every finger had a ring on it.

Goni, the young man, smiled and obediently began to pluck out a tune on his battered guitar. The instrument was at least twice as old as he was and had seen better days, but it played well enough. It was his prized possession, and he was rarely seen without it.

He was dressed like the girl, with multiple layers, but less dramatically. His purple hair was cut short on the sides and left long on top, and he wore a vest over a sweater riddled with holes, much like his shoes and pants.

There were no words to any of his music, but Marieni knew all his songs. As he played on, she began to make up lyrics, waxing poetic about the feeling of travelling through tunnels deep into the Earth. In her imagination the tunnels travelled all over the Earth, branching off in hundreds of different directions. She liked to think that they were created by mysterious beings, whose only purpose was to dig tunnels from one city to another, to connect the Earth in an unseen harmony and help bring us all closer together.

Goni smiled at her words as his fingers moved from chord to chord. When he finished, he reached out for the remainder of her joint, but before she could hand it to him, the fire escape began to shake. They both looked up, curious as to who was coming out of the gallery so late at night, but they couldn't see anyone. Still the stairs continued to shake, as if someone were climbing down. Rising to his feet, Goni forgot all about the joint. He narrowed his eyes as he tried to see who was coming towards them, but there was only darkness. Actually, it was worse than darkness. The light near the back door should have illuminated the railing or the stairs, but it was obstructed by a large dark void that seemed to block out any light that might exist. A large, dark void that was drawing closer and closer.

Words escaped him as he reached out for Marieni, his hand closing around her upper arm.

"We need to go," he whispered.

She didn't seem to hear him, staring up at the darkness with a confused expression on her face. She didn't understand how it could be making such a commotion with its movements since it seemed to be made of swirling smoke. She tried to read its aura but there was only darkness.

The darkness seemed to stop and look at them, gaining shape and form, growing larger and more solid as they stared. A giant mouth opened, and sharp white teeth glistened in the moonlight. Goni felt his heart rise in his throat as two glowing red eyes looked down at them.

AFTERWORD
by MATTHEW LEDREW

Five years ago I wrote a tiny novella for spite. It was a novel with a few different cool ideas that I had been really, really jazzed about at the time, but the glue that had held them together was spite. There had been a lot of backlash against genre fiction involving vampires at the time, and I had just gotten turned onto the local queerlit scene (and there are a few other influences I'd like to keep to myself), but the glue that held them together was a very negative emotion.

The novel that came from that was *Jacobi Street*, and as of this writing it is one of my favorite things I have ever produced. It's fun and paints a complete world in a little artist community. It involves so many characters I've met in my time in the arts, their points of view, their posturing and their passion. And it wasn't a part of a series. I'm a writer who writes in long, multi-book narratives, so the idea of taking a break and writing a one-off was appealing: and I could say all I needed to say all at once. It could be cathartic.

But immediately, that part of my brain that asks, "Okay, what next?" at the end of every Xander Drew novel or Infinity novel perked up and asked the same as I was finishing *Jacobi Street*. "Okay, but... what next?" Nothing, it's done. "Ha. No really, but what next?" Nothing. It's a one-off novel in the Engen Universe. "Cool cool. Cool cool, cool. But, let me ask you this: what next?"

Eventually I caved to my worse impulses, as I always do when at the keyboard. I wrote a scene to end the novella where the threat from the first ended up at a theatre on Jacobi Street: The Quaint Little Theatre, in fact. And then I closed the book on the novel and went about my life. When it came time to seek publication I sent the book out to peers that I trusted – Amanda Labonté, Paul Carberry, and Ali House – for thoughts and blurbs.

Ali House is one of the most talented authors I know. When she wrote back that she loved the book, that it reminded her of those same little artist communities we both hailed from, I was ecstatic. And then at the end she asked about that scene at The Quaint Little Theatre.

"So about the end, you left it open for a sequel at a theatre, and I love that," she said.

"Um... sure." And I realized in that moment I had. And in that moment I knew, whole and complete, the broad stokes of the sequel. *Dammit*. This was supposed to be an escape from multi-book series for me!

"I need to talk to you when you write it. Because I'm a theatre brat, and nothing – *nothing* – makes me more upset than when I read theatres written wrong. I need you to give me that draft when you're done it, so that I can read it and make sure it's actually like a theatre. A real theatre. Because I'm sick of the way media portrays theatres. I'm a giant theatre brat. I am far too obsessed with theatres. Theatres, swords, cyanide, and happiness. Those are the things I enjoy." Some of that wasn't actually said, but the gist is there. We chatted for hours, and as we did her ideas started to slot into the *very* loose idea that I'd had for what a sequel would look like. They glommed on and, after a while, it became more hers than mine. Her ideas were sticking, and mine were falling off.

"This is your book," I said. I remember looking at my schedule of things to write – *As Loved Our Fathers, Garden of the Eighth Circle, First Aid* – and realizing how long it would take me to write a follow-up in The Quaint Little Theatre even if I'd had the drive to. Even if it wasn't already *hers*.

"Pardon?" she asked. I imagine her head tilted back. She does that.

"You are the best author I know. You should write this. This is your theatre book, just like *Jacobi Street* was my arts community book."

And I told her then what I'm telling you now: Ali House is one of the greatest authors I have ever had the pleasure of reading, let alone working with. I told her I wouldn't write a follow-up, that I was more excited for *her* follow-up than my own. That she was the only one who could do it, whose voice could manage it. She said that she'd try.

She did a fucking amazing job, I think you'll agree.

Thank you, Ali House, for writing *Variety Show*, and making my world a little brighter in the process. I adore it, and you. Looking forward to many years of novels and friendship in the future.

ENGEN TIMELINE

With over twenty-five novels spread over multiple series by many different authors, the Engen Universe of titles is growing every day and into genres we couldn't have imagined! From the original ten book *Coral Beach Casefiles* thriller series, its crime novel sequel series *Xander Drew*, our flagship science-fiction thiller title *Infinity*, or single-novels like *Jacobi Street* and *Exposure*, there's something in the Engen Universe for everyone with more books by more authors on the way soon!

...But how do the events relate to one another, chronologically? While some astute readers have guessed at the potential timeline (some accurately, some not), we're going to finally set the question of the Engen Timeline to rest.

Turn the page for an up-to-date guide of the ever-widening world of Engen, featuring the works of Ali House, Ellen Curtis, Erin Vance, Matthew Daniels, Andrea Hackett, Sarah Thompson, Jay Paulin, and Matthew LeDrew!

In the 10 Years Prior Black September

"Reptilia" by Matthew LeDrew
published in *light | dark*.
Danger descends on a small secluded town
in the form of a deadly virus with fantastic
and terrible side-effects. Can a small group of
doctors escape alive?

Compendium by Ellen Curtis
Three short stories forming the basis for the
Engen Universe's ties to suspense, genetic
engeneering, and the supernatural. Features
the stories "The Tourniquet Revival," "Falling
into Fire" and "At Midnight, the Dawn."

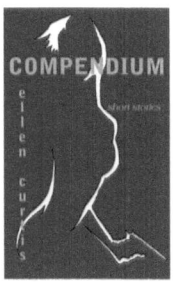

"The Theogony" by Matthew LeDrew
published in *light | dark*.
A tale of young Theo Flaherty of the *Infinity*
series and his time admitted against his will to
the Black Springs hospital, where he learns to
paint, and seeks out his father.

Black September

"Revving Engen" by Matthew LeDrew
published in *light | dark*.
A direct lead-in to both *Infinity* and *Black
Womb*, Tasha travels to Coral Beach, Maine on
a hot tip about a recently discovered young
man with incredible abilities.

Infinity by Ellen Curtis & Matthew LeDrew
Faced with a destiny he's uncertain of, the enigmatic Victor must bring together four unique people with very special abilities… or face the tasks ahead alone. Guaranteed to excite!

Black Womb by Matthew LeDrew
Fifteen years ago, something happened in Coral Beach, Maine that resulted in the present death of a seventeen-year-old boy. Now four high-school students must try to solve the mystery… before the killer picks them off.

Jacobi Street by Matthew LeDrew
When a mysterious painting shows up at an art gallery he works at, Bob must work with Eddie and Sloan to track down its sinister origins and convince the people living on Jacobi Street of them, before its too late!

Transformations in Pain by Matthew LeDrew
When two girls are assaulted and one is hospitalized, the residents of Coral Beach must put their shared tragedies behind them and stop the man responsible, as well as unlock the secrets behind the true nature of the Womb…

Year One: October

Variety Show by Ali House
Local performer Wendy is introduced to the
drama and mystique of The Quaint Little
Theatre of Jacobi Street. But backstabbing
aren't the only dangers at play in this venue...

Smoke and Mirrors by Matthew LeDrew
The approaching trial of Genblade brings
closure to the people of Coral Beach, until
people start showing up dead in the same
manner they did when he was at large.

"Scarlett" by Andrea Hackett
published in *light | dark*.
Introducing Scarlett, the slightly damaged
hunter on a mission to save others from the
monsters from her past.

"The Inevitable" by Ali House
published in *The Lightbulb Forest*
A young woman must contend with the
emergence of a frightening new power
alongside the emotional high of a first date.

The Tourniquet Reprisal by Curtis & LeDrew
A man lives in Atlanta, Georgia that people don't talk about, but everyone knows he's there. He arrived a year ago and turned a gaggle of uneducated youth into something new, something to fear.

Roulette by Matthew LeDrew
As the teen suicide rate in Coral Beach starts to climb astronomically fast, Xander travels to Los Angeles to fight his most terrifying adversary yet… and learns that the only thing worse than looking for release… is finding it.

Year One: November

Exodus of Angels by Curtis & LeDrew
Victor's enigmatic past is illuminated when Jaycee accompanies him to visit a new friend in the paliative care ward of the Black Springs hospital, where Theo also happens to be searching for a cure for Leigh.

Ghosts of the Past by Matthew LeDrew
Coral Beach faces its most awesome threat when one of Engen's past mistakes is unleashed upon the unsuspecting populous. Friends and enemies unite to fight a common enemy… but will even that be enough?

Touch Your Nose by Matthew LeDrew
Simon Monk must infiltrate the San Fransico branch of Shane Industries, a massive company with deep ties to the Engen Universe. Where do his true loyalties lie? And can he get out without causing harm?

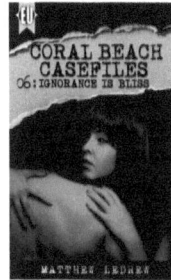

Ignorance is Bliss by Matthew LeDrew
After being set through the ringer one too many times, Xander decides that his life with Julie needs a little more attention… which is bad news because a new villain has come to town with his sights set on Adam Genblade.

"Gristle While You Work" by Jay Paulin published in *light|dark*.
A short story centering around the rise of a new, and possibly cannibalistic, serial killer in the Engen Universe.

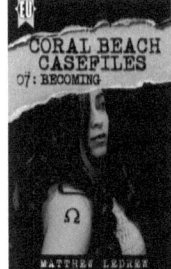

Becoming by Matthew LeDrew
For months Xander Drew has been doing his level best to keep the streets of Coral Beach clean, which means it's time for the forces of darkness to strike back… all at once.

Inner Child by Matthew LeDrew
Julie is hospitalized with life-threatening wounds to both body and soul. But the real threat comes from the hospital walls themselves, as a demonic presence makes itself known to Xander and his friends.

End of Year One

Gang War by Matthew LeDrew
The Tees, a homicidal gang of evil men, has finally been taken down by Xander Drew. But his victory is short lived, as retired Tees are mysteriously killed. With a town of suspects, anyone can be the culprit... including one of their own.

Chains by Matthew LeDrew
Sociopath Derek Smith has been freed from prison and is praying on the weak; and none are weaker than August Styles: a pregnant girl with Down Syndrome who has run away from home.

"Omega" by Ellen Curtis
published in *light | dark*.
A sinister division of Engen begins a series of experiments on pregnant women in a fashion eerily similar to those that created the original Black Womb project.

The Long Road by Matthew LeDrew
Xander meets the American people — and realizes that the world is harsh and wicked, but can also be soft and gentle, even loving. Xander Drew comes of age on the road, and sets his new direction.

Year Two

Cinders by Matthew LeDrew
Detective Horton enters a violent and dangerous world he didn't know existed beneath the veneer of order and structure that he has based his entire deductive method around.

Sinister Intent by Matthew LeDrew
One of the killers Detective Horton could not catch has resurfaced: a serial killer who flaunts his sinister intent in front of the Los Angeles Police Department, making it so that no one is safe.

Faith by Matthew LeDrew
Xander's mysterious and troublesome past returns to haunt him on the streets of Los Angeles; a place where even more people can get caught in the crossfire of the games of death and deceit that makes up his life.

Flickers in the Night by Matthew LeDrew
Lisa Rowdan is hunted by her haunting --
and powerful -- ex-boyfriend Ryan through a
lonely city street. Can she escape him?
One of over twenty great sprine-tingling short
stories!

Garden of the 8th Circle by Curtis & LeDrew
Victor brings Chad, Abby, and Alice into a
dangerous conflict a decade in the making,
fighting an out of control cult for the fate of a
young soul. Meanwhile, Theo investigates a
mysterious event in Los Angeles.

Family Values by Matthew LeDrew
Xander and his new friends Crowley, Lisa, and
Tim investigate a series of kidnappings and
murders that stretch back decades, all of which
have the same similar twist: victims being
found after years of being missing.

Fate's Shadow by Matthew LeDrew
When one of Xander's old cases comes up
for trial, Megan Greene returns with it. The
former friends are led into conflict regarding
her client's innocence. However, they put
their difference aside when they both become
targets of the vigilante known as Shiro Gilbert.

First Aid by Matthew LeDrew
Xander takes his feud with mob boss Stephen Fields to the streets, and his attracts the attention of the *Infinity* team. Before the arrive, he'll have pushed the mob boss into an all out gang war, the likes of which the city will never recover from.

Exposure by Erin Vance
Joshua Deering just wanted was to pass his final photography project. But that's not what happened. But hindsight is 20/20, and now creepy cemetery guy Adrian, Josh, and Josh's two friends are being stalked by nameless, violent strangers.

The Future

"Remers" by Sarah Thompson
published in *light | dark*.
In the not-too-distant future of the Engen Universe, young athletes are the targets of a scouting program to create the next stage of super soldier with cybernetic enhancements.

DARK STORIES FROM ENGEN BOOKS

THE HOWL BECONS

Growing up without his father, Tyler had no way of knowing the horrible secret that has plagued his family for generations. To free himself and find the cure, he will have to look beyond himself and into his dark history.

"A very ambitious novel… the horrors of everyday life can be worse than anything in fiction. The idea of using werewolves as a metaphor – to me this pushes the book a bit above much of what is out there… Brad [Dunne] is a very good writer and obviously has a deep background."
— Andrew Peacock

WESTON'S WAR

Something evil grows in the heart of Colorado. Bill Weston was a man of the West. He knew it – its land, its people, its stories. It was where he plied his trade, hunting men for money. His life wasn't easy, but it was predictable. That all changed when he captured Faraway Sue and he was led on a trip through the Colorado forests

"Take a little Zane Grey. Add a little Penny Dreadful. Read with Sam Elliot's voice. Discover Jon Dobbin's masterful The Starving."
— Darrell Power,
Great Big Sea

Zombies have taken over!
#1 Bestseller!

Zombie hordes created by the evil Pharmakon company have taken over the world, including the one place that always thought it was safe from the calamities of the outside: the quiet, scenic shores of Newfoundland's west coast. In this horrifying first volume, the island of Newfoundland is besieged by zombies and are left unprepared for the massacres that follow, struggling to stay alive as the city of Corner Brook falls to the undead hordes...

Book One: Outbreak (Feb 2017)
Book Two: The Viking Trail (Dec 2017)
Book Thee: Republic of Newfoundland (Sept 2019)

"[Carberry] draws in his readers from the first page, effortlessly providing the tension and fear necessary to create his terrifying apocalyptic tale."
— *Fiona Cooke Hogan, author of* What Happened In Dingle

"This is an astonishing first novel from Paul Carberry. I read it over the course of two days, and in those two days my time was divided thusly: reading it, and wishing I were still reading it."
— *Matthew LeDrew, author of* Black Womb

ABOUT THE AUTHOR

Ali House is an award-winning, bestselling author, originally from Newfoundland. She is a graduate of the Fine Arts program at Sir Wilfred Grenfell College (MUN), and currently resides in Halifax where she works in arts administration and spends more time than a person should in and around theaters. She is a master storyteller whose work has helped define the landscapes of science-fiction, fantasy, and horror writing in Atlantic Canada.

To date, House's short fiction has appeared in every volume of the *From the Rock* anthology series, as well as *Bluenose Paradox, Kit Sora Artobiography,* and *Terror Nova.* Her short fiction was collected in 2020 in *The Lightbulb Forest.*

Previous novels include *The Six Elemental* and *The Fifth Queen,* both a part of her creator-owned *Segment Delta Archives* series. Other works include the fantasy series *Choose Your Own Adventurer,* the *Santa Claus Protection Program,* and *The Island Adventure* as a part of the Slipstreamers series of novellas.

Variety Show is her sixth novel.

www.ingramcontent.com/pod-product-compliance
Lightning Source LLC
Chambersburg PA
CBHW032116020726
47494CB00007BA/2091